AN EMOTION OF GREAT DELIGHT

A Novel

TAHEREH MAFI

ALSO BY
TAHEREH MAFI

A Very Large Expanse of Sea

AN EMOTION OF GREAT DELIGHT

A Novel

TAHEREH MAFI

Published in the USA in 2021 by HarperCollins Children's Books,
a division of HarperCollins*Publishers*, 195 Broadway, New York, NY 10007, USA

First published in Great Britain 2021 by Electric Monkey, part of Farshore
an imprint of HarperCollins*Publishers*
1 London Bridge Street, London SE1 9GF

farshore.co.uk

HarperCollins*Publishers*
1st Floor, Watermarque Building, Ringsend Road, Dublin 4, Ireland

Text copyright © Tahereh Mafi 2021
The moral rights of the author have been asserted.

ISBN 978 1 4052 9826 1
Printed in Great Britain by CPI Group
1

A CIP catalogue record for this title is available from the British Library

Typeset by Avon DataSet Ltd, Arden Court, Alcester, Warwickshire B49 6JN

Stay safe online. Any website addresses listed in this book are correct at the time
of going to print. However, Farshore is not responsible for content hosted by third
parties. Plea   websites
can contai   hildren

DECEMBER

2003

ONE

The sunlight was heavy today, fingers of heat forming sweaty hands that braced my face, dared me to flinch. I was stone, still as I stared up into the eye of an unblinking sun, hoping to be blinded. I loved it, loved the blistering heat, loved the way it seared my lips.

It felt good to be touched.

It was a perfect summer day out of place in the fall, the stagnant heat disturbed only by a brief, fragrant breeze I couldn't source. A dog barked; I pitied it. Airplanes droned overhead, and I envied them. Cars rushed by and I heard only their engines, filthy metal bodies leaving their excrement behind and yet—

Deep, I took a deep breath and held it, the smell of diesel in my lungs, on my tongue. It tasted like memory, of movement. Of a promise to go somewhere, I released the breath, anywhere.

I, I was going nowhere.

There was nothing to smile about and still I smiled, the tremble in my lips an almost certain indication of oncoming hysteria. I was comfortably blind now, the sun having burned so deeply into my retinas that I saw little more than glowing orbs, shimmering darkness. I laid backward on dusty asphalt, so hot it stuck to my skin.

I pictured my father again.

His gleaming head, two tufts of dark hair perched atop his ears like poorly placed headphones. His reassuring smile that everything would be fine. The dizzying glare of fluorescent lights.

My father was nearly dead again, but all I could think about was how if he died I didn't know how long I'd have to spend pretending to be sad about it. Or worse, so much worse: how if he died I might not have to pretend to be sad about it. I swallowed back a sudden, unwelcome knot of emotion in my throat. I felt the telltale burn of tears and squeezed my eyes shut, willing myself to get up. Stand up.

Walk.

When I opened my eyes again a ten-thousand-foot-tall police officer was looming over me. Babble on his walkie-talkie. Heavy boots, a metallic swish of something as he adjusted his weight.

I blinked and backed up, crab-like, and evolved from legless snake to upright human, startled and confused.

"This yours?" he said, holding up a dingy, pale blue backpack.

"Yes," I said, reaching for it. "Yeah."

He dropped the bag as I touched it, and the weight of it nearly toppled me forward. I'd ditched the bloated carcass for a reason. Among other things, it contained four massive textbooks, three binders, three notebooks, and two worn paperbacks I still had to read for English. The after-school pickup was near a patch of grass I too-optimistically frequented, too often hoping someone in my family would remember I existed and spare me the walk home. Today, no such luck. I'd abandoned the bag and the grass for the empty parking lot.

Static on the walkie-talkie. More voices, garbled.

I looked up.

Up, up a cloven chin and thin lips, nose and sparse lashes, flashes of bright blue eyes. The officer wore a hat. I could not see his hair.

"Got a call," he said, still peering at me. "You go to school here?" A crow swooped low and cawed, minding my business.

"Yeah," I said. My heart had begun to race. "Yes."

He tilted his head at me. "What were you doing on the ground?"

"What?"

"Were you praying or something?"

My racing heart began to slow. Sink. I was not devoid of a brain, two eyes, the ability to read the news, a room, this man stripping my face for parts. I knew anger, but fear and I were better acquainted.

"No," I said quietly. "I was just lying in the sun."

The officer didn't seem to buy this. His eyes traveled over my face again, at the scarf I wore around my head. "Aren't you hot in that thing?"

"Right now, yes."

He almost smiled. Instead he turned away, scanned the empty parking lot. "Where are your parents?"

"I don't know."

A single eyebrow went up.

"They forget about me," I said.

Both eyebrows. "They forget about you?"

"I always hope someone will show up," I explained. "If not, I walk home."

The officer looked at me for a long time. Finally, he sighed.

"All right." He backhanded the sky. "All right, get going. But don't do this again," he said sharply. "This is public property. Do your prayers at home."

I was shaking my head. "I wasn't—" I tried to say. *I wasn't,* I wanted to scream. I wasn't.

But he was already walking away.

TWO

It took a full three minutes for the fire in my bones to die out.

In the increasing quiet, I looked up. The once-white clouds had grown fat and gray; the gentle breeze was now a chilling gust. The drunk December day had sobered with a suddenness that bordered on extreme and I frowned at the scene, at its burnt edges, at the crow still circling above my head, its *caw caw* a constant refrain. Thunder roared, suddenly, in the distance.

The officer was mostly memory now.

What was left of him was marching off into the fading light, his boots heavy, his gait uneven; I watched him smile as he murmured into his radio. Lightning tore the sky in two and I shivered, jerkily, as if electrocuted.

I did not have an umbrella.

I reached under my shirt and tugged free the folded newspaper from where I'd stashed it in my waistband, flush against my torso, and tucked it under my arm. The air was heavy with the promise of a storm, the wind shuddering through the trees. I didn't really think a newspaper would hold up against the rain, but it was all I had.

These days, it was what I always had.

There was a newspaper vending machine around the corner from my house, and a few months ago, on a whim, I'd purchased a copy of the *New York Times*. I'd been curious about Adults Reading the Newspaper, curious about the articles therein that sparked the conversations that seemed to be shaping my life, my identity, the bombing of my friends' families in the Middle East. After two years of panic and mourning post-9/11, our country had decided on aggressive political action: we had declared war on Iraq.

The coverage was relentless.

The television offered a glaring, violent dissemination of information on the subject, the kind I could seldom stomach. But the slow, quiet business of reading a newspaper suited me. Even better, it filled the holes in my free time.

I'd started shoving quarters in my pocket every day, purchasing copies of the newspaper on my way to school. I perused the articles as I walked the single mile, the exercise of mind and body elevating my blood pressure to dangerous heights. By the time I reached first period I'd lost both my appetite and my focus. I was growing sick on the news, sick of it, heedlessly gorging myself on the pain, searching in vain for an antidote in the poison. Even now my thumb moved slowly over the worn ink of old stories, back and forth, caressing my addiction.

I stared up at the sky.

The lone crow overhead would not cease its staring, the weight of its presence seeming to depress the air from my lungs. I forced myself to move, to shutter the windows in my mind as I went. Silence was too welcoming of unwanted thoughts; I listened instead to the sounds of passing cars, to the wind sharpening against their metal bodies. There were two people in particular I did not want to think about. Neither did I want to think about looming college applications, the police officer, or the newspaper still clenched in my fist, and yet—

I stopped, unfurled the paper, smoothed its corners.

Afghan Villagers Torn by Grief After US Raid Kills 9 Children

My phone rang.

I retrieved it from my pocket, going still as I scanned the flashing number on the screen. A blade of feeling impaled me—and then, just as suddenly, withdrew. *Different number.* Heady relief nearly prompted me to laugh, the sensation held at bay only by the dull ache in my chest. It felt as if actual steel had been buried between my lungs.

I flipped open the phone.

"Hello?"

Silence.

A voice finally broke through, a mere half word emerging

from a mess of static. I glanced at the screen, at my dying battery, my single bar of reception. When I flipped the phone shut, a prickle of fear moved down my spine.

I thought of my mother.

My mother, my optimistic mother who thought that if she locked herself in her closet I wouldn't hear her sobs.

A single, fat drop of water landed on my head.

I looked up.

I thought of my father, six feet of dying man swaddled in a hospital bed, staring into the middle distance. I thought of my sister.

A second drop of rain fell in my eye.

The sky ruptured with a sudden *crack* and in the intervening second—in the heartbeat before the deluge—I contemplated stillness. I considered lying down in the middle of the road, lying there forever.

But then, rain.

It arrived in a hurry, battering my face, blackening my clothes, pooling in the folds of my backpack. The newspaper I lifted over my head endured all of four seconds before succumbing to the wet, and I hastily tucked it away, this time in my bag. I squinted into the downpour, readjusted the demon on my back, and pulled my thin jacket more tightly around my body.

Walked.

LAST YEAR

PART I

Two sharp knocks at my door and I groaned, pulled the blanket over my head. I'd been up late last night memorizing equations for my physics class, and I'd gotten maybe four hours of sleep as a result. The very idea of getting out of bed made me want to weep.

Another hard knock.

"It's too early," I said, my voice muffled by the blanket. "Go away."

"Pasho," I heard my mother say. *Get up.*

"Nemikham," I called back. *I don't want to.*

"Pasho."

"Actually, I don't think I can go to school today. I think I have tuberculosis."

I heard the soft *shh* of the door pushing open against carpet, and I curled away instinctively, a nautilus in its shell.

I made a pitiful sound as I waited for what seemed inevitable—for my mother to drag me, bodily, out of bed, or, at the very least, to rip off the covers.

Instead, she sat on me.

I nearly screamed at the unexpected weight. It was excruciating to be sat upon while curled in the fetal position; somehow my stacked bones made me more vulnerable to damage. I thrashed around, shouted at her to get off me, and she just laughed, pinched my leg.

I cried out.

"Goftam pasho." *I said get up.*

"How am I supposed to get up now?" I asked, batting away the sheets from my face. "You've broken all my bones."

"Eh?" She raised her eyebrows. "You say that to me? Your mother"—she said all this in Farsi—"is so heavy she could break all your bones? Is that what you're saying?"

"Yes."

She gasped, her eyes wide. "Ay, bacheyeh bad." *Oh, you bad child.* And with a slight bounce, she sat more heavily on my thighs.

I let out a strangled cry. "Okay okay I'll get up I'll get up oh my God—"

"Maman? Are you up here?"

At the sound of my sister's voice, my mom got to her feet. She whipped the covers off my bed and said, "In here!" Then, to me, with narrowed eyes: "Pasho."

"I'm pasho-ing, I'm pasho-ing," I grumbled.

I got to my feet and glanced, out of habit, at the alarm clock I'd already silenced a half dozen times, and nearly had a stroke when I saw the hour. "I'm going to be late!"

"Man keh behet goftam," my mom said with a shrug. *I told you.*

"You told me nothing." I turned, eyes wide. "You never told me what time it was."

"I did tell you. Maybe your tuberculosis made you deaf."

"Wow." I shook my head as I stalked past her. "Hilarious."

"I know, I know, I'm heelareeus," she said with a flourish of her hand. She switched back to Farsi. "By the way, I can't take you to school today. I have a dentist appointment. Shayda is taking you instead."

"No I'm not," my sister called, her voice growing louder as she approached. She popped her head inside my room. "I have to leave right now, and Shadi isn't even dressed."

"No— Wait—" I startled scrambling. "I can be dressed in five minutes—"

"No you can't."

"Yes I can!" I was already across the hall in our shared bathroom, applying toothpaste to my toothbrush like a crazy person. "Just wait, okay, just—"

"No way. I'm not going to be late because of you."

"Shayda, what the hell—"

"You can walk."

"It'll take me forty-five minutes!"

"Then ask Mehdi."

"Mehdi is still asleep!"

"Did someone say my name?"

I heard my brother coming up the stairs, his words a little rounder than usual, like maybe he was eating something as he spoke. My heart gave a sudden leap.

I spat toothpaste into the sink, ran into the hall. "I need a ride to school," I cried, toothbrush still clenched in my fist. "Can you take me?"

"Never mind. I've gone suddenly deaf." He barreled back down the stairs.

"Oh my God. What is wrong with everyone in this family?"

My dad's voice boomed upward. "Man raftam! Khodafez!" *I'm leaving! Bye!*

"Khodafez!" the four of us shouted in unison.

I heard the front door slam shut as I flew to the banister, caught sight of Mehdi on the landing below.

"Wait," I said, "please, please—"

Mehdi looked up at me and smiled his signature, devastating smile, the kind I knew had already ruined a few lives. His hazel eyes glittered in the early-morning light. "Sorry," he said. "I've got plans."

"How do you have plans at seven thirty in the morning?"

"Sorry," he said again, his lean form disappearing from view. "Busy day."

My mom patted me on the shoulder. "Mikhasti zoodtar pashi." *You could've woken up earlier.*

"An excellent point," Shayda said, swinging her backpack over one shoulder. "Bye."

"No!" I ran back into the bathroom, rinsed my mouth, splashed water on my face. "I'm almost ready! Two more minutes!"

"Shadi, you're not even wearing pants."

"What?" I looked down. I was wearing an oversize T-shirt. No pants. "Wait— Shayda—"

But she was already moving down the stairs.

"Manam bayad beram," my mom said. *I have to go, too.* She shot me a sympathetic glance. "I'll pick you up after school, okay?"

I acknowledged this with a distracted goodbye and darted back into my room. I changed into jeans and a thermal at breakneck speed, nearly stumbling over myself as I grabbed socks, a hair tie, my scarf, and my half-zipped backpack. I flew downstairs like a maniac, screaming Shayda's name.

"Wait," I cried. "Wait, I'm ready! Thirty seconds!"

I hopped on one foot as I pulled on my socks, slipped on my shoes. I tied back my hair, knotted my scarf à la Jackie O— or, you know, a lot of Persian ladies—and bolted out the door. Shayda was at the curb, unlocking her car, and my mom was settling into her minivan, still parked in the driveway. I waved at her, breathless as I shouted—

"I made it!"

My mom smiled and flashed me a thumbs-up, both of which I promptly reciprocated. I then turned the wattage

15

of my smile on Shayda, who only rolled her eyes and, with a heavy sigh, granted me passage in her ancient Toyota Camry.

I was euphoric.

I waved another goodbye at my mom—who'd just turned on her car—before depositing my unwieldy bag in Shayda's back seat. My sister was still buckling herself into the driver's side, arranging her things, placing her coffee mug in the cup holder, et cetera, and I leaned against the passenger side door, taking advantage of the moment to both catch my breath and enjoy my victory.

Too late, I realized I was freezing.

It was the end of September, the beginning of fall, and I hadn't yet adjusted to the new season. The weather was inconsistent, the days plagued by both hot and cold stretches, and I wasn't sure it was worth risking Shayda's wrath to run upstairs and grab my jacket.

My sister seemed to read my mind.

"Hey," she barked at me from inside the car. "Don't even think about it. If you go back in the house, I'm leaving."

My mom, who was also a mind reader, suddenly hit the brakes on her minivan, rolled down the window.

"Bea," she called. *Here.* "Catch."

I held out my hands as she tossed a balled-up sweatshirt in my direction. I caught it, assessed it, held it up to the sky. It was a standard-issue black hoodie, the kind you pulled over your head. Its only distinguishing features were the drawstrings, which were a vibrant blue.

"Whose is this?" I asked.

My mom shrugged. "It must be Mehdi's," she said in Farsi. "It's been in the car for a long time."

"A long time?" I frowned. "How long is a long time?"

My mom shrugged again, put on her sunglasses.

I gave the cotton a suspicious sniff, but it must not have been abandoned in our car for too long, because the sweater still smelled nice. Something like cologne. Something that made my skin hum with awareness.

My frown deepened.

I pulled the sweatshirt over my head, watched my mom disappear down the drive. The hoodie was soft and warm and way too big for me in the best way, but this close to my skin that faint, pleasant scent was suddenly overwhelming. My thoughts had begun to race, my mind working too hard to answer a simple question.

Shayda honked the horn. I nearly had a heart attack.

"Get in right now," she shouted, "or I'm running you over."

DECEMBER

2003

THREE

When it rained like this people often shot me knowing glances and friendly finger-guns, said things like, "Lucky you, eh? Einstein over here doesn't even need an umbrella," finger-gun, finger-gun, eyebrow waggle. I'd always smile when someone said something like this to me, smile one of those polite smiles that held my mouth firmly shut. I never understood this assumption, this idea that my scarf was somehow impervious to water.

It was discernibly not.

My scarf was discernibly not neoprene; it did not resemble vinyl. It was silk, an intentional choice, not just for its weight and texture but for the sake of my vanity. Silk caressed my hair during the day, made it smooth and shiny by the time I got home. That anyone thought my hijab capable of withstanding a thunderstorm was baffling to me, and yet it was a logic maintained by a surprisingly large number of people.

If only they could see me now.

The rain had drenched my scarf, the skin of which was now plastered to my head. Water ran in rivulets down the sides of my neck, my hair heavy, dripping. A few rebellious strands had come loose, harsh winds whipping them across my eyes, and though I made to tuck them away, to pull myself together, my efforts were more habit than hopeful. I was no fool. I knew I was going to die of pneumonia today, possibly before my next class even started.

I was a senior in high school but on Monday and Wednesday evenings I took a multivariable calculus class at the local community college. It was the equivalent of taking an AP class. The units were transferrable, helped inflate my GPA.

My parents were into it. Most parents were into it.

But my parents, like many Middle Eastern mothers and fathers, *expected* it. They expected me to take multivariable calculus as a senior in high school the way they expected me to become a doctor. Or a lawyer. A PhD would also be accepted, though with decidedly less enthusiasm.

I looked up again, at the opposition.

The rain was falling harder now, faster, but there was no time to take shelter. If I wanted to get to class on time, I had to be walking now. I knew I'd spent too long after school hoping someone would come get me, but I couldn't help it; my hope was greater on Mondays and Wednesdays. Greater because I hoped for more than a ride home—I wanted to be spared the long walk to the college, two and a half miles away.

I was tempted to skip.

The temptation was so palpable I felt a tremble in my spine. I imagined my sodden bones carrying me straight home and my heart stuttered at the thought, happiness threatening. Cars flew past me, spraying me with dirty water, and I wavered further, shivering in soaked jeans and sopping shoes. I was a smudge with a dream, standing at a literal crossroads. I dreamed of going left instead of right. I dreamed of hot tea and dry clothes. I wanted to go home, home, wanted to sit in the shower for an hour, boil my blood.

I couldn't.

I couldn't miss class because I'd already missed a day last month, and missing two days would drop my grade, which would hurt my GPA, which would hurt my mother, which would break the single most important rule I'd made in my life, which was to become so innocuous a child as to disappear altogether. It was all for my mother, of course. I was ambivalent about my father, but my mother, I didn't want my mother to cry, not for me. She cried enough for everyone else these days.

I wondered then whether she'd look out the window, whether she'd be reminded, in a rare moment, of her youngest child, of my pilgrimage to calculus. My father, I knew, would not. He was either asleep or watching reruns of *Hawaii Five-0* on a television stapled to a partition. My sister would certainly not be bothered, not with anything. No one else I knew would even know to come for me.

Last year, my mother would've come.

Last year, she would've known my schedule. She would've

called, checked in, threatened my sister with violence for abandoning me to the elements. But in the wake of my brother's death my mother's soul had been rearranged, her skeleton reconfigured. The crushing waves of grief that once drowned me had begun, slowly, to ebb, but my mother— Over a year later my mother still seemed to me not unlike sentient driftwood, bobbing along in the cool, undiluted waters of agony.

So I'd become a ghost.

I'd managed to reduce my entire person to a nonevent so insignificant my mother seldom even asked me questions anymore. Seldom realized I was around. I told myself I was helping, giving her space, becoming one less child to worry about—mantras that helped me ignore the sharp pain that accompanied the success of my disappearing act.

I only hoped I was right.

A sudden gust of wind rattled through the streets, pushing me back. I'd no choice but to duck my head against the gust, the motion exposing my open collar to the rain. A tree trembled overhead and a stunning, icy torrent of water shot straight down my shirt.

I audibly gasped.

Please, God, I thought, *please please don't let me die of pneumonia.*

My socks were soup, my teeth chattering, my clenched fingers growing slowly numb. I decided to check my cell phone for a sign of life, mentally sorting through the short list of people I might be able to call for a favor—but by the time I fished the metal brick out of the marsh of my pocket it was waterlogged and glitching. Never mind pneumonia, I would likely die of electrocution. My future had never looked so bright.

I smiled at my own joke, my lips curving toward insanity, when a car sped by so quickly it just about bathed me in runoff. I stopped then, stopped and stared at myself, at my amphibious state. It was unreal how I looked. I couldn't possibly go to school like this, and yet I would, I would, propelled forward by some greater scruple, some nonsense that gave my life meaning. It all suddenly struck me as ridiculous, my life, so ridiculous I laughed. Laughed and then choked, having aspirated a bit of sewer water. Never mind. Never mind, I was wrong; I would die of neither pneumonia nor electrocution. Asphyxiation would usher the angel of death to my door.

This time I did not laugh.

The speeding car had come to a complete and sudden stop. Right there, right in the middle of the slick road. The taillights came on, white and bright, and the car idled for at least fifteen seconds before making a decision. Tires squealing, it reversed in the empty street, skidding to a terrifying halt beside me.

Wrong again.

Not pneumonia, not electrocution, not asphyxiation, no— Today, I was going to be murdered.

I stared up at the sky again.

Dear God, I thought, *this was not what I meant when we last spoke.*

FOUR

I stood stock-still and waited, waited for the window to roll down, for my future to be determined. Waited for fate.

Nothing happened.

Seconds passed—several and then a dozen—and nothing, nothing. The silver car idled beside me, its heavy, glistening body dripping steadily into dusk. I waited for its driver to do something. Anything.

Nothing.

I couldn't quell my disappointment. In the breathless interlude, my curiosity had grown greater than my fear, which now felt perilously close to something like anticipation. This near-denouement was the closest I'd been to excitement since the day I thought my father would die, and bonus: the car looked warm. At least death, I thought, would be warm. *Dry.*

I was ready to ignore everything I'd ever learned about getting into cars with strangers.

But this was taking too long.

I squinted into the rain; I couldn't see much from where I stood, just darkened windows and exhaust fumes. It was a short distance from the sidewalk to the car, and I wanted to clear that distance, wanted to knock on the car's window, demand an explanation. I was stopped short by the sound of trapped, muted voices.

Not talking—*arguing*.

I frowned.

The voices grew louder, more agitated. I approached the car like a crescent moon, my back curved against the rain, head bowed toward the passenger door. I had no way of being entirely certain of my fate today, but if I really was going to be murdered I wanted to get it over with. I squelched the three steps across the sidewalk, adjusted my sopping headscarf, and waved at the dark window of the strange car. I might've even smiled. My trembling, secret hope was that the driver was not a murderer, but a kind Samaritan. Someone who'd seen me drowning and wanted to help.

The car sped away.

Without warning—its tired engine revving a little too hard—it sped away, bathing me anew in sewer water. I stood there dripping on the sidewalk, skin burning with unaccountable embarrassment. I couldn't make sense of it, couldn't understand how I'd just been appraised and rejected by a murderer. A murdering duo, even.

It occurred to me, briefly, that the car had seemed familiar, that the driver might've been someone I knew. This thought was not comforting to me, and yet it was a clinging thought, one that could not, at this hour, be probed sufficiently for truth. I shook my head, shook the congealing hypothesis from my mind. The sky was going gray, and silver Honda Civics were ubiquitous; I couldn't be sure of anything.

I lifted one wet foot, then the other.

Of all things, I had the Toys R Us jingle stuck in my head, and I hummed it as I walked, as I passed faceless shopping malls and gas stations. I kept humming it until it became a part of me, until it became the disorienting background music for the PowerPoint presentation of disappointments looping behind my eyes.

I saw that Honda Civic again when I finally got to school.

It was parked there in the parking lot, and I dripped past it on my way toward the main building. The rain had stopped, but it was nearly dark now, and I was nearly dead. Right now I had only enough functioning brain matter to keep my teeth from chattering, but I couldn't stop myself from staring at that Honda Civic as I walked onto campus, my neck turned at a comically uncomfortable angle. I was trying to look more closely at the car, but the sky seemed to have sunk down, sat on the ground. Everything and everyone was gray. I moved through clinging mist, couldn't really see where I was going.

Metaphors, everywhere.

I tried not to think about my throbbing head or the blue tint to my skin. I tried to focus, even with the fog. Now, perhaps more than before, I wanted to understand what had happened. I wanted to know who drove that car and whether I really did know the driver. I was trying to understand why the car had pulled over without murdering me. I was trying to suppress the panic in my chest that wondered whether I was being followed.

And then I fell.

There were stairs leading up to the school, stairs I'd climbed a thousand times, and yet tonight I didn't, couldn't see them. I fell onto them instead, indenting skin and bones and catching myself with slippery hands. My head only just grazed the stone and I was grateful, but I'd slammed my knee pretty hard and could feel it bleeding.

I rolled over onto my back, my backpack; closed my eyes. Cold wind skated over the planes of my face, chilled my damp clothes. I couldn't stop laughing. Mine was the mute variety, the kind betrayed only by the curve of my smile, the shaking of my shoulders. Pain was fracturing up my leg; I felt it in my neck. I didn't want to get up. I wanted to lie here until someone carried me out, carried me away.

I wanted my mother.

Dear God, I thought. *Why? Why why why?*

I sighed, opened my eyes to the sky. And with a single,

herculean effort, I pushed myself upright. I wasn't going to class tonight. But I wasn't going home, either.

I decided to stay awhile, steep in my failures. Today had been disappointing on so many levels; I figured I might as well go all in, toss all twenty-four hours in the trash, start over tomorrow. I should take advantage of the rain, I thought, take advantage of my destroyed clothes, I thought, take advantage of the quiet, the silence, and the opportunity to sin in peace.

FIVE

The school was fairly well lit at night, well enough to see without being seen. I found my familiar spot, planted my wet bag on the wet concrete, and rooted around in my things with shaking hands.

I was ruthless with my hands.

I scraped my knuckles against stone, drew blood, cut my palms on cardboard, drew blood. I shoved those same hands in pockets and held my breath as they throbbed. I didn't bandage cuts. I ignored burns. When I looked at my hands I was presented with the evidence of my station: bruises untended, scrapes unhealed.

I was unnoticed except in the worst ways.

As far as the larger world was concerned, I was about as remarkable as a thumb. My presence was notable only occasionally and only because my face seemed familiar to people—familiar the way fear was familiar, the way dread was familiar. Everywhere I went strangers squinted at me, minds buffering for all of half a second before they placed my entire person in a box, taped it shut.

Adults were always seeking me out—why? why?—to ask me direct and specific questions about international relations as if I were some kind of proxy for my parents, for their home country, for some larger answer to a desperate question. As if my seventeen-year-old body were old enough to understand the complexities of any of this, as if I were a seasoned politician whose tenuous connection to a Middle Eastern country I rarely visited would suddenly make me an expert in politics. I didn't know how to tell people that I was just as stupid today as I was yesterday, and that I spent most of my time thinking about how my life was falling apart in ways that had nothing to do with the news cycle. But there was something about my hijab that made people disregard my age, made me seem like fair game.

We were, after all, at war with people who looked just like me.

I unearthed my damp newspaper along with my damp cigarettes, tucked a cylinder between my lips, dropped the paper in my lap, and zipped my backpack shut. I stretched out my injured leg, grimacing as I reached for the lighter in my pocket.

It took a few tries, but when the butane finally caught, I took a moment to stare at the flame. I'd spun the spark wheel enough times that it had abraded the pad of my thumb.

I took a deep drag, held it in, let it go, sat back, stared up. I couldn't see the stars.

On the one hand, smoking was not cool. Smoking would kill you. Smoking was a vile, disgusting habit I did not condone.

On the other hand—

Dear God, I thought, exhaling the poison. *Would you please just kill my father already? I can't take the suspense.*

I picked up the paper, stared at the melting headline.

When I read the newspaper I saw myself, my family, and my faith reflected back at me as if in a fun-house mirror. I felt a hopelessness building in my chest every day, this desperation to tell someone, to shake strangers, to stand on a park bench and scream—

There's no such thing as an Islamic terrorist.

It was morally impossible—philosophically impossible—to be Muslim and a terrorist at the same time. There was nothing in Islam that condoned the taking of innocent lives. And yet there it was, every day, every day, the conflation: Muslim terrorist. Islamic terrorist.

The Middle East, our president had said, was the axis of evil.

I saw the latent danger in the storytelling, the caricature we were becoming, two billion Muslims quickly solidifying into a faceless, terrifying mass. We were being stripped of gradation, of complexity. The news was turning us into monsters, which made us so much easier to murder.

I pinched the cigarette between my thumb and forefinger, held it up against the sky. I hated how much I enjoyed this disgusting pastime. Hated how it seemed to steady me, befriend me in my darkest hours. I could already feel the fist unclench in my chest and I relished it, closing my eyes as I took another drag, this time exhaling the smoke across the wilting article. The piece was about the recklessness of our airstrikes on Afghan villages, about how our military intelligence appeared questionable; hundreds of innocent Afghans were killed in the search for Al Qaeda members who never materialized. I'd read the last paragraph a thousand times.

> *"The Americans are all the time making these mistakes,"*
> *said Mr. Khan, whose two sons, Faizullah, 8, and*
> *Obeidullah, 10, were killed. "What kind of Al Qaeda*
> *are they? Look at their little shoes and hats. Are they*
> *terrorists?"*

"Wow."

The voice came from the fog, from outer space. It was a single word but it startled me with its heft and depth, with its fullness. It had been hours since I'd spoken to anyone but a police officer, and I seemed to have forgotten how sounds sounded.

Nerves spiked through me.

Hastily, I put out the cigarette, but I knew it was too late, knew there was no denying any of this. I would be eighteen in six weeks, but right now that didn't matter. Right now I was seventeen years old, and what I was doing was illegal. Stupid.

But then the stranger laughed.

The stranger laughed and my fear froze, my heart unclenched. I experienced relief for all of two seconds before I caught a glimpse of his face. He'd stepped into the severe light of a streetlamp and my eyes focused, unfocused; my soul fled my body. I felt it then—knew, somehow, even then, that I would not survive this night unchanged.

He wouldn't stop laughing.

"My dear sister in Islam," he said, affecting horror. "*Astaghfirullah*. This is shameful."

Mortification was a powerful chemical. It had dissolved my organs, evaporated my bones. I was loose flesh splayed on concrete.

He did not seem to notice.

He placed a hand on his chest, continued the show. "A young sister in hijab," he said, *tsk*ing as he towered over me. "Alone, late at night. Smoking. What would your parents—" He hesitated. "Wait. Are you bleeding?"

He was staring at my knee, at the tear in my jeans. A dark stain had been spreading slowly across the denim.

I dropped my face in my hands.

An arm reached for my arm, waited for my cooperation. I did not cooperate. He retreated.

"Hey, are you okay?" he said, his voice appreciably gentler. "Did something happen?"

I lifted my head. "I fell."

He frowned as he studied me; I averted my eyes. We were now positioned under the same shaft of light, his face so close to mine it scared me.

"*Jesus*," he said softly. "My sister is such an asshole."

I met his gaze.

He took a sharp breath. "All right, I'm taking you home."

That rattled my brain into action. "No, thank you," I said quickly.

"You're going to die of pneumonia," he said. "Or lung cancer. Or"—he shook his head, made a disapproving noise—"depression. Are you seriously reading the newspaper?"

"It helps me de-stress."

He laughed.

My body tensed at the sound. Ancient history wrenched open the ground beneath me, unearthing old caskets, corpses of emotion. I hadn't talked to him in over a year—hadn't been this close to him in over a year—and I wasn't sure my heart could handle being alone with him now.

"I already have a ride home," I lied, staggering upright. I stumbled, gasped. My injured knee was screaming.

"You do?"

I closed my eyes. Tried to breathe normally. I felt the weight of my dead cell phone in my pocket. The weight of the entire day, balanced between my shoulder blades. I was freezing. Bleeding. Exhausted.

I knew no one was coming for me.

My shoulders sagged as I opened my eyes. I sighed as I looked him over, sighed because I already knew what he looked like. Thick brown hair so dark it was basically black. Deep brown eyes. Strong chin. Sharp nose. Excellent bone structure. Eyelashes, eyelashes, eyelashes.

Classically Persian.

He rolled his eyes at my indecision. "I'm Ali, by the way. I'm not sure if you remember me."

I felt a flash of anger. "That's not funny."

"I don't know," he said, looking away. "It's a little funny." But his smile had vanished.

Ali was my ex–best friend's older brother. He and his sister, Zahra, were the two people I did not want to think about. My memories of them both were so saturated in emotion I could hardly breathe around the thoughts, and barreling face-first into my past wasn't helping matters in my chest. Even now, I was barely holding it together, so assaulted were my senses by the mere sight of him.

It was almost cruel.

Ali was, among other things, the kind of handsome that transcended the insular social circles frequented by most members of Middle Eastern communities. He was the kind of good-looking that made white people forget he was terrorist-adjacent. He was the kind of brown guy who charmed PTA moms, dazzled otherwise racist teachers, inspired people to learn a thing or two about Ramadan.

I'd once hated Ali. Hated him for so effortlessly straddling the line between two worlds. Hated that he seemed to pay no price for his happiness. But then, for a very long time, I didn't.

Didn't hate him at all.

I sighed. My tired body needed to lean against something or else start moving and never stop, but I could presently do neither. Instead, I sat back down, folding myself onto the concrete with all the grace of a newborn calf. I picked up the forgotten lighter off the ground, ran my thumb over the top. Ali had gone solid in the last thirty seconds. Silent.

So I spoke. "Do you go to school here now?"

He was quiet a moment longer before he exhaled, seemed to come back to himself. He shoved his hands in his pockets. "Yeah."

Ali was a year older than me, and I'd thought for sure he'd go out of state for college. Zahra rarely fed me details on her brother's life, and I'd never dared to ask; I just assumed. The Ali I'd known had been effortlessly smart and had big plans for his future. Then again, I knew how quickly things could change. My own life was unrecognizable from what it was a year ago. I knew this, and yet I couldn't seem to help it when I said—

"I thought you got into Yale?"

Ali turned. Surprise brightened his eyes for only a second before they faded back to black. He looked away again and the harsh lamplight rewarded him, casting his features in stark, beautiful lines. He swallowed, the slight, near-imperceptible movement sending a bolt of feeling through my chest.

"Yeah," he said. "I did."

"Then why are y—"

"Listen, I don't really want to talk about last year, okay?"

"Oh." My heart was suddenly racing. "Okay."

He took a deep breath, exhaled a degree of tension. "When did you start smoking?"

I put down the lighter. "I don't really want to talk about last year, either."

He looked at me then, looked for so long I thought it might kill me. Quietly, he said, "What are you doing here?"

"I take a class here."

"I know that. I meant what are you doing *here*"—he nodded at the ground—"soaking wet and smoking cigarettes?"

"Wait, how do you know I take a class here?"

Ali looked away, ran a hand through his hair. "Shadi, come on."

My mind went blank. I felt suddenly stupid. "What?"

He turned to face me.

He met my eyes with brazen defiance, almost daring me to look away. I felt the heat of that look in my blood. Felt it in my cheeks, the pit of my stomach.

"I asked," he said.

It was both a confession and a condemnation; I felt the weight of it at once. It was suddenly clear that he'd asked Zahra about me, about my life—even now, after everything.

I had not. I'd tried instead to forget him entirely, and I'd not succeeded.

"Listen," he said, but his voice had gone cold. "If you already have a ride, I'll leave you alone. But if you don't, let me drive you home. You're bleeding. You're shivering. You look terrible."

My eyes widened at the insult before the rational part of my brain even had a chance to process the context, but Ali registered his mistake immediately. Spoke in a rush.

"I didn't— You know what I mean. You don't look terrible. You look—" He hesitated, his eyes fixed on my face. "The same."

I felt death bloom bright in my chest. I'd always been the kind of coward who couldn't survive even the vaguest suggestion of a compliment.

"No. You're right." I gestured to myself. "I look like a drowned cat."

He didn't laugh.

I'd learned, recently, that some people thought I was beautiful. Moms, mostly. The moms at the mosque loved me. They thought I was beautiful because I had green eyes and white skin and because a huge swath of Middle Eastern people were racist. They were blithely unaware of the fact; had no idea that their unabashed preference for European features was shameful. I, too, had once been flattered by this kind of praise, just until I learned how to read a history book. Beyond this select group of undiscerning moms, only one person had ever told me I was beautiful—and he was standing right in front of me.

With some difficulty, I got to my feet. The pain in my knee

had begun to ebb, but my body had stiffened in the aftermath. Carefully, I bent my joints. Rubbed my elbows.

"Okay," I said finally. "I would appreciate the ride."

"Good call."

Ali stalked off; I followed.

He led me straight to his car without so much as a backward glance, and suddenly it was right there, right in front of me: the silver Honda Civic I'd seen before.

The one that nearly killed me.

LAST YEAR

PART II

My concerns over the hoodie had been mostly forgotten. The steadily plummeting temperatures forced me to abandon my reservations and focus, instead, on my gratitude for the extra layer.

I shivered when the lunch bell rang.

I stood up, gathered my things, pulled on my backpack. It was much warmer inside the school than outside it, but even with artificial heating I remained on the edge of uncomfortable, huddling deeper into the soft material. I pushed into the crowded hallway and tugged the too-long sleeves over my hands, crossed my arms against my chest. It seemed unlikely that the sweatshirt belonged to anyone but Mehdi, but even if it didn't—who would know? It was the most ubiquitous variety of black hoodie. I was definitely overthinking this.

Still, I couldn't deny the frisson of feeling that moved

through me at the thought of the alternative: that the sweatshirt belonged to someone else, to someone I knew, to someone strictly off-limits to me.

I took an unsteady breath.

Zahra and I had only one class together this semester, and since I'd been running late this morning, we hadn't yet crossed paths. Our parents still carpooled a couple days a week, but our previously braided schedules had begun, slowly, to part, and I wasn't sure what that meant for us. More than anything else, I felt uncertainty.

Every day it seemed like she and I were teetering on the edge of something—something that wasn't necessarily good—and it made me nervous. I often felt like I was walking on eggshells around Zahra, never certain what I might do to upset her, never certain what kind of emotional turbulence she might introduce to my day. It made everything feel like an ordeal.

I didn't know how to fix it.

I didn't know how to say something about the tension between us without sounding accusatory. Worse, I worried she might leverage any perceived slight into an excuse to shut me out. There was a great deal of history between us—layers and layers of sediment I dearly treasured—and I didn't want to lose what we had. I wanted only for us to evolve backward, into the versions of ourselves that never caught fire when we collided.

I cried out.

Someone had slammed into me, knocking the air from my lungs and the thoughts from my head. The stranger muttered an insincere *Sorry* before shoving past, and I shook my head, deciding then to stop fighting the tide. I needed to drop off some books at my locker before I joined Zahra in our usual spot, but it felt like the whole school had a similar idea. We were all of us heading to the locker bays.

I was still moving at a glacial pace when I became aware of a gentle pressure at the base of my spine. I felt the heat of his hand even through the hoodie, his fingers grazing my waist as they drew away. The simple contact struck a match against my skin.

"Hey," he said, but he wasn't looking at me. He was smiling into the crowd, watching where he was going.

"Hi." I could no longer remember feeling cold.

Ali glanced in my direction. His hand had abandoned me but he leaned in when he said—without meeting my eyes—

"Are you wearing my hoodie?"

I nearly stopped in place. Twin gusts (pleasure, mortification) blew through me, and then, dominating all else—

Panic.

Eventually, the bottleneck broke. We'd arrived at my locker. I dropped my backpack to the floor, spun around to face him, felt the metal frame press against my shoulder blades. Ali was staring at me with the strangest look on his face, something close to delight.

"I didn't know this was yours," I said quietly. "My mom found it in her car."

He touched one of the bright-blue drawstrings, wound it around his finger.

"Yeah," he said, meeting my gaze. "This is mine."

A wash of heat colored my cheeks and I closed my eyes as if it made any difference, as if I could stop us both from seeing it.

"I'm sorry," I said. "I didn't know."

"Hey, don't apologize, I don't—"

Carefully, without disturbing my scarf, I pulled the hoodie over my head and handed it to him, practically shoved it at him.

"Shadi." He frowned, tried to give it back. "I don't care if you wear it. You can have it."

I was shaking my head. I didn't know how to say even a little bit without saying everything. "I can't."

"Shadi. Come on."

I turned around, turned the combination on my locker. Wordlessly, I unzipped my backpack, swapped out my books.

Ali moved closer, bent his head over my shoulder. "Keep it," he said, his breath touching my cheek. "I want you to keep it."

I felt my body tense with a familiar ache, a familiar fear. I couldn't move.

"Hey."

I straightened at the sound of Zahra's voice.

"Hi," I said, forcing myself to speak. My heart was now racing for entirely new reasons.

Zahra stepped closer. "What are you guys doing?" Then, to me, with an approximation of a laugh: "Why did you just give my brother your sweater?"

"Oh. My mom actually found it in her car this morning."

Zahra frowned. My answer was not an answer.

"I, um, thought it belonged to Mehdi," I amended. "But it belongs to Ali. I was just giving it back to him."

Zahra looked at Ali—whose face had shuttered closed. He glanced at me before he shoved a hand through his hair, balled the sweatshirt under his arm.

"I'll see you later," he said to no one, and disappeared into the crowd.

Zahra and I stood in silence, watching him go. My heart would not cease racing. I felt as if I were standing, in real time, in front of a ticking bomb.

Boom.

"What the fuck, Shadi?"

I tried to explain: "I didn't know it was his. I was running late and I'd forgotten my jacket and—"

"Bullshit."

"Zahra." My heart was pounding. "I'm not lying."

"How long have you been doing this?"

"What? Doing what?"

"This, Shadi, *this*. Hooking up with my brother."

"Hooking up with . . ." I blinked, my head was spinning. "I'm not . . ."

"Was that what you were doing last night? Were you out with my brother?"

I was shaking my head, certain this was some kind of nightmare. "I was doing my physics homework."

"God, you're unbelievable," she said. "Fucking unbelievable."

A few heads turned for the second time, passersby always surprised to hear a girl in hijab swearing loudly in the hall.

I lowered my voice a few octaves in an effort to compensate. "There is literally nothing going on between me and Ali. I swear to God. I swear on my life."

Zahra was still livid, her jaw tensed as she stared at me. But she'd at least stopped yelling, which gave me hope.

"I swear," I said, trying again. "I had no idea the hoodie was his. It was a crazy morning, and I was rushing around so much I forgot to grab my jacket, and my mom found his sweatshirt in her car. Ali must've forgotten it at some point. We all thought it was Mehdi's."

Zahra looked at me for a long time, and though I was the one holding my breath, she was the one who finally exhaled.

Slowly—very slowly—the tension left her body.

When her anger broke, she looked suddenly close to tears. "You're really not hooking up with my brother?"

"Zahra, come on. Can you even imagine? Listen to yourself."

"I know. *I know.*" She sniffed, wiped her eyes. "Ugh, I'm

sorry. You're right. I'm sorry. He'd never even be interested in someone like you."

"Exactly." What?

"I mean, no offense or anything." She shot me a look. "But you're definitely not his type."

I tried to smile. "I'm no one's type. Most people take one look at me and run screaming in the opposite direction."

She laughed.

I was only half kidding.

Suddenly, Zahra dropped her face in her hands. "I'm sorry. I'm just—" She sighed. Shook her head. "I'm sorry."

"Hey," I said, squeezing her shoulder. "Can we just forget this whole thing? Please? Let's get some lunch."

She took a deep breath. Let it go.

We left.

I only realized later that she'd never answered my question.

DECEMBER

2003

SIX

I couldn't believe it.

I gave the silver car a wide berth, wouldn't move any closer. The wind was pushing against my legs, shoving cold up my sleeves, but I was frozen in place, looking from him to the Honda.

Finally, finally, Ali turned to face me.

"That was you?" I asked.

He had the decency to look ashamed. "My sister takes a chem class here a couple nights a week."

I already knew that.

"My mom makes me drive her."

This was now obvious.

"I saw you drowning in the rain," he said, finally getting to the point. "I wanted to offer you a ride."

"But you didn't."

He inhaled deep. "Zahra wouldn't let me."

I was staring at my shoes now, at the shattered remains of a leaf trapped in my laces.

I was stunned.

"You didn't even have an umbrella," Ali was saying. "But she just—I don't know. I didn't understand. I still don't get what happened between you guys."

This was so much. Too much to unpack.

Several months ago, when we officially declared war on Iraq, most of my friends started crying. I was devastated, too, but I kept my head down. I didn't argue with people who didn't seem to understand that Saudi Arabia and Afghanistan and Iraq were all very different countries. I said nothing when my history teacher's army reserve unit got called up, said nothing when he stared at me while making the announcement.

I didn't know why he stared at me.

It was like he wanted something from me, either an apology or a show of gratitude, I wasn't sure. I wrote nothing but my name in the card we gave him at his going-away party.

Hate crimes were on the rise.

Muslim communities were in turmoil. Women were taking off their scarves, guys changing their names. People were freaked out. Our mosques were bugged, set on fire. Last month we found out that Brother Farid—Brother Farid, the guy always volunteering and helping out, the guy so beloved he was invited to a half dozen weddings last year—was an undercover FBI agent.

Heartbreak.

It was a time of change, turbulence, shifting sands. People were making names for themselves, even the most useless teenagers blooming into activists and advocates for change. Heretofore nobodies rallied for grassroots organizations, organized peace talks.

I was growing weary of everyone.

I hated the posturing at the mosque, the competitions to prove piousness in the face of persecution. I hated the gossip meant to shame the women who'd taken off their hijabs. People were particularly vicious to the older women, said they were all uglier sans scarves, decrepit. *What's the point of taking it off when you're that old?* people would ask, and laugh, as if a woman's motivations to put on a hijab had anything to do with making herself more or less attractive. As if anyone had any right to judge another person's fear.

Zahra had taken off her scarf.

Zahra, who'd been my best friend for years. Two months ago she stopped wearing hijab and stopped talking to me, too. Cut me out of her world—effectively shattered my heart—without further explanation. She wouldn't even look at me at school anymore, didn't want to be associated with me. From the outside, her reasons seemed obvious.

I knew better.

I knew Zahra hadn't thrown away six years of friendship because of a single sea change. She'd hid the truth in another truth; we'd split for a Russian nesting doll of reasons. But this—tonight—to discover that she harbored this level of hatred toward me, this kind of anger—

I felt physically ill.

"I'm really sorry," Ali was saying, when he hesitated. "Actually, I don't know why I'm apologizing. I didn't do anything wrong."

"No," I said. "No, you didn't."

Something wet landed on my cheek and I looked up, eyelashes fluttering against the unexpected drizzle. A sharp wind shook up a pile of dead leaves, wrapped around my ankles. It smelled like decay.

"We should get going," Ali said, his eyes following mine upward. He had a hand on the roof of his car, a hand on the driver door. "Don't worry about Zahra, okay? I usually wait in the library while she's in class, catch up on homework. I'll come back for her."

"Okay." Rain dribbled down my cheeks, dripped from my lips.

I didn't move.

Ali laughed, then frowned. Looked at me like I'd lost my mind.

Perhaps I had. Tentacles of fear had suddenly reached up my throat, driven into my skull. I had turned to stone. I'd felt it suddenly, felt it like a bullet to the chest, cold and solid and real—

Something terrible had happened.

"You okay?" Ali opened the driver's side door; rain blew

sideways into the car. "Seriously, I'm sorry about my sister. I think she's just going through a lot right now."

I heard a phone ring, distantly, miles away.

"Is that yours?" I heard myself say.

"What?" He closed the car door. "My what?"

"Your phone. Ringing."

Ali's frown deepened, a furrow bordering on irritation. "My phone isn't ringing. No one's phone is ringing. Listen—"

I was staring at a single windshield wiper on Ali's silver Honda Civic when my dead phone rang with a shrillness that broke the night, my paralysis.

I answered it.

At first I couldn't hear my sister's voice. At first I heard only my heart pound, heard only the wind. I heard my name the third time she screamed it, heard everything she said after that. My older sister was hysterical, screaming half-formed thoughts and incomplete information in my ear and I tried to listen, tried to ask the right follow-up questions, but the cell phone fell from my shaking hand, snapped when it hit the ground.

I'd gone blind. I heard my own breathing, loud in my head, heard my blood moving, fast in my veins.

Ali did not get to me before I fell. He dove to the pavement half a beat later, caught my head before it cracked. He was saying something, shouting something.

Please, God, I thought. *Dear God,* I thought. *Please, God,* I thought.

"Shadi? *Shadi*—"

I came back to my body with a sudden gasp. I sat on trembling legs, steadied myself with trembling arms. My eyes were wild; I could feel it, could feel them dilate, dart back and forth, focus on nothing.

"What's going on?" he was saying. "What just happened?"

I was looking at the ground.

I remember it, remember the way the wet pavement glittered under the streetlamp. I remember the smell of dirt, the damp press of silk against my cheek. I remember the way the branches shook, the way my body did.

"I need you to drive me to the hospital," I said.

SEVEN

Ali did not look at me while we drove. He did not speak.

I did not feel his eyes on me, did not feel him move more than was absolutely necessary to perform his task.

I looked at myself.

Somehow I'd multiplied, one iteration sitting in the passenger seat, the other running alongside the car, peering in the window.

The first thing I noticed was the cut on my chin. Freshly serrated skin, bright red blood smeared across my jaw. My silk scarf was once pale green, shiny; it was now a dull slate, pockmarked with fresh water stains. I'd chosen this scarf because I knew it complimented my eyes and because I was impractical. Silk scarves were an older woman's game; few girls my age cared for the slippery material, opting instead for basic cottons, polyesters. Fabric that stayed in place with little fuss.

I was an idiot in many ways, it had turned out.

My scarf had been pushed back and forth enough times that it had bunched in places, shifted backward. My dark hair was pitch-black when wet, loose strands wild around my face, curling with damp. I was always pale, but today my pallor was deathly. I looked gaunt. My eyes were bigger, greener than usual. Glazed.

I did not think I was ugly. But I also did not think I would rate mention were it not for my eyes—for my irises—for the cold, sharp green of that which is not yet grown. I'd inherited my unripe eyes from my father, and some days I found it hard not to resent them both.

I became aware of my eyes in earnest last year, about the time my mother started locking herself in her closet. I became aware of my eyes because others had become aware of my eyes. My face. My body. So many women—always the women, only the women—talked about me, dissected me, my skin, my waist, the size of my feet, the slope of my nose, my eyes my eyes my eyes.

By the time I turned seventeen I'd definitively shed the wild awkwardness expected of most teenagers my age. This was right around the time my mother would not stop crying, around the time I'd lie awake in bed and pray to God to kill my father. I stopped laughing so loudly, stopped running around so recklessly, stopped smiling, generally.

I had aged.

People thought I was growing up, and perhaps I was,

perhaps *this* was growing up—*this, this*, an uncertain spiral into a darkness lined with teeth.

My sadness had made me noteworthy. Beautiful. Had imbued in me a kind of dignity, a weight I could not uncarry. I knew this because I heard it all the time, heard it from old ladies at the mosque who praised me for my still lips, my folded hands, my reluctance to smile. They'd declared me demure, a good Muslim girl with fair skin, light eyes. My mother had since received five marriage proposals from other mothers, their grown sons standing behind them, beaming.

My mother threatened to move away. Threatened to leave the mosque. Damned the other women to hell, stormed through the house slamming doors. *She's only seventeen*, she'd scream.

A child.

I didn't remember walking into the hospital. I didn't remember parking or opening the car door. I didn't notice, not right away, when Ali came with me, said nothing when he lied to the nurse, assuring her that yes, we were siblings, and yes, the patient was our mother.

Our mother.

Not *my* mother. Not *my* mother, not my *mother*, my mother, who was supposed to be at home staring listlessly at the wall or else singing terribly melodramatic Persian songs off-key in the kitchen. My mother was young, relatively healthy, the one who never got sick and never, ever took time off for herself. This was a clerical error, a mistake made by God or maybe this guy, the one wearing blue scrubs and a Dora the Explorer lanyard, the one squinting at his computer screen in search of my mother's room number. It was my father who was meant for this place, this fate. My father who'd earned the right to be murdered by his own heart and for whom I waited, with baited breath, for a similar phone call, for a summons to such a place, for a justice still overdue.

Dear God, I thought, *this is not funny.*

I saw my sister at the exact moment the Dora the Explorer lanyard stopped bobbing up and down. I felt, but did not see, when the nurse looked up, said something—a floor, a room number—

"Where the hell have you been?" Shayda said, marching up to me, her long, dark blue scarf billowing around her. I had the strangest thought as I watched her move, as the long lines of her manteau rippled in the air. The thought was so strange I nearly laughed. *You look like a jellyfish*, I wanted to say to her. Tentacles and elegance. No heart.

"Where is she?" I said instead. "What happened?"

"She's fine," my sister said sharply. "We're waiting on some paperwork, and then we can leave."

I nearly sank to the floor. I looked around for a place to fall apart, for a seat or an unoccupied corner, and made it only as far as the wall, at which I stared. There was a terror in my throat so large I could not swallow.

I turned around.

I needed to move, I wanted to see my mother, I wanted answers and reasons to sleep tonight, but my nerves would not settle. I stared at my sister with wide eyes, wings beating in my chest.

"Hey, you okay?" Ali said gently, reminding me he was there.

I looked up at him, not seeing him.

Shayda made a sound in her throat, something like disbelief. I swung my head around, blinked. Her irritation dissolved, evolved as she took me in, analyzed the mess. "So this is why you didn't answer your phone? Too busy doing whatever you two were doing"—she shot a disgusted look at Ali—"to care that your mother is in the hospital?"

"What?" Ali said, stepping forward. "That's n—"

I was still staring at my sister when I held up a hand to stop him. It was meant to be a gesture only, a signal. But he walked straight into my open palm, broad chest pressed against my splayed fingers. I felt warm cotton, a shallow valley, hard and soft planes.

I pulled my hand away.

Our eyes did not meet.

"Don't worry about her," I said quietly.

My mom hated it when my sister and I fought, so I rarely rose to the bait these days, but cutting out the petty fights had left us with little else. When we weren't fighting, we seldom had reason to speak. I always thought it would help matters to ignore her, and yet, for some reason, my silence only drove my sister crazier. Even now I could see her anger building, her body tensing.

"What are you even doing here?" Shayda said, turning on Ali. "You know people might see you standing next to us, right? They might think you know us. Or—*gasp*—they might think you're Muslim."

Ali frowned. "What are you—"

"Please. Don't engage with her. Please just ignore her."

Shayda practically exploded.

"What do you mean, *just ignore her*? When was the last time you saw him at the mosque, Shadi? When was the last time he said a single word to either of us? Or to Maman and Baba? Last month he saw Maman at the store and she'd only talked to him for a minute or two—nothing more—but apparently it was too much. He left the store after that. Walked out the door. *He abandoned his grocery cart in the middle of the aisle* so he wouldn't have to bump into her again. Can you even believe that?"

I looked at Ali, but he wouldn't meet my eyes. He stared at the wall instead—stared at a blank, bright wall with a barely contained anger I'd never even known him to possess. I couldn't process this right now. Not right now.

My mother was in the hospital.

I turned back around. "Shayda— Please—"

"Why are you even with him? He doesn't associate with people like us anymore. His reputation can't handle it."

I felt Ali move before I saw the motion. He stalked toward

my sister, looking suddenly murderous, eyes flashing. I could tell he was about to say something and I nearly shouted just to beat him to it.

"Stop," I said. "Shayda, you're yelling at the wrong person. *Please.* Please just tell me what happened. I couldn't understand what you said on the phone. Is she hurt? How did she get here? Did you have to call an ambulance?"

Fear flitted in and out of Shayda's face, giving her away. Her eyes shone, then dulled, the only evidence of the war within her, and in that moment she transformed. She was suddenly more than my stupid sister—she was the sister I loved, the sister for whom I would cut off an appendage, take a bullet. I pulled her into my arms even as she stiffened, held on tight when she softened. I heard the hitch in her breath.

"Whatever it is, it's going to be okay," I whispered, and she flinched. Jerked back. Became a stranger.

"Why do you smell like cigarettes?"

Panic rioted through me.

Lie, I screamed at myself. *Lie, you idiot.*

"That's my fault," Ali said, and I spun around, stunned. His anger was gone, but in its absence he looked wrung-out. Run-down. "My bad."

"You smoke now?" Shayda again. "That's disgusting. And *haram.*"

"Really?" he asked, eyebrows up. "I thought it was a gray area."

Shayda's eyes darkened. "Whatever. You can go now."

Ali didn't move. He looked away from Shayda, his eyes glancing off the wall, the ceiling, the floor. But he didn't move.

He looked at me.

"Are you sure you want me to go? Do you guys even have a ride home?"

"Shayda has her car," I explained.

"What about your dad? Do you want me to call him?"

I was still processing that, still trying to find a tidy way to explain that my father was likely sleeping in a room not unlike the one my mother currently occupied when he said—

"What about Mehdi? Did h—"

Ali froze, as suddenly as if he'd been struck by lightning. Slowly, he dragged both hands down his face.

"*Fuck*," he breathed. Squeezed his eyes shut. "I'm sorry. I'm sorry."

Shayda walked away.

She left, left without a word, the lines of her lean form rippling in the distance. Me, I'd fossilized in place. I stood staring at a single flickering bulb in the brightly lit corridor long after she disappeared from sight. My sister was wrong about many things, but she was at least partly right about one: Ali didn't associate with us anymore.

It was surreal how it happened, surreal how different my life had become in his absence. Ali and I, Shayda and Zahra— we used to see each other every day. My first year of high school we'd all carpool, our moms taking turns driving us to and from campus. Once Ali and Shayda got their own cars they tore free, only too happy to break up the band, pursue their independence. Still, my life kept colliding into his. His life kept colliding into mine. Ali and I had been fixtures in each other's lives for five years until one day, a week before my brother died, everything between us broke. We stopped talking at the beginning of my junior year, his senior year.

Overnight, we'd become strangers.

"Shadi."

I looked up.

"I'm sorry," he whispered. "I'm—"

I shook my head too fast. "Oh, Ali. It's okay." I smiled and realized I was crying, my eyes bleeding slow tears that made no sound. My emotions had finally boiled over. I didn't know why they chose that moment, didn't know why they were directed at him; but I knew, even then, even as I could do nothing about it, that the picture I made must've been terrifying.

Ali looked struck; he stepped forward.

I walked away.

EIGHT

The teakettle was screaming.

I stared at it, the steam curling, silver body shuddering on the stovetop, demanding attention. We had an old electric stove, its white paint chipping in places, burned-on grease splattered across the steel drip-bowls within which sat lopsided heating elements. The lopsided heating elements made it so that nothing heated evenly, which made it impossible to cook anything properly on this stove, which was one of the quiet shames of my family. The only thing this stove ever did well was bring water to an acceptable boil.

I turned down the heat. Poured the hot water from the kettle into the waiting belly of a porcelain teapot, brewing the leaves within. I wrapped the whole thing in a hand towel, set it aside, let it steep. We didn't have a proper samovar, so this would have to suffice.

I heard murmurs of conversation coming from the living room, where my mother and my sister were waiting. I did, did not want to join them, did, did not want to know what they were discussing. I lingered in the kitchen too long, arranging cookies on a plate, selecting glasses for our tea.

My mother had thought she was having a heart attack.

Shayda was at the house when it happened, called 911. She'd called me, too, apparently, several times, but my dying phone had connected only once. The ambulance came, drove straight to our home for the third time in as many weeks, strapped my mother to a stretcher, and wheeled her away. A lamp had been knocked over, small things had been disarranged. There was dirt on the rug from their boots, the paramedics, dirt from their boots and their equipment.

The sight had sent a cold shudder through my body.

My mother had thought she was having a heart attack, and I could see why. My father had just had two, both of them in the same month. She'd seen and heard him describe, at length, the symptoms, the possible warning signs.

The doctor ran all kinds of tests on her, but they came back negative. She had not had a heart attack, he'd said.

She'd had a panic attack.

She was going to be fine. They'd given her something, some drug she would no doubt have refused had she known exactly what was in it, but it helped calm her down. Helped steady the horrible stutter in her heart.

For some reason, the doctor had thought I was the eldest.

He didn't even ask, he'd just assumed, and he'd motioned for me to follow him out into the hall, closed my mother's door behind him. Shayda had gone to pull the car around. My mother was changing back into her clothes. The doctor grimaced as he turned to me, grimaced and said—

"You're the older sister, right? Listen, there's something I need to discuss with you about your mom."

Perhaps I should've told him the truth. There was no doubt a reason he wanted to speak with the oldest child, no doubt a legal or moral or psychological reason why I was uniquely unqualified, as the youngest, to hear what he was about to say. But my terrified curiosity would not allow me to walk away from an opportunity to know more about my mother. I wanted to know what was happening to her. I *needed* to know.

At first, the doctor said nothing.

Finally, he sighed. "I noticed your father is here in the hospital, too."

"Yes."

He tried to smile. "You okay?"

Heat pushed up my throat, the backs of my eyes, seared the roof of my mouth. I swallowed. Swallowed. "Yes," I said.

He looked down at his clipboard, looked back up. Sighed again. "Does your mother have a history of depression?"

I blinked at the doctor, at the dark scruff growing down his neck, at the surgical mask stuffed into his coat pocket. He wore a scuffed gold band on his ring finger, and in that hand he clenched a stethoscope. There was a smudge of something on his shirt, chocolate or blood, I couldn't tell. I didn't know what his eyes looked like. I couldn't meet them.

I did not understand.

"When your brother died," he said, and I looked up then, took the hit to the chest, felt it shudder through my bones. "When your brother died did she"—he frowned—"has she been—has it been hard for her? Harder than what might seem normal?"

The question was so stupid it struck me hard across the face.

The doctor backpedaled, apologized, tried again. "There's no right way to say this. I've never had to have this conversation with the child. Usually I have these conversations with the parent." He took a breath. "But I feel that, considering the circumstances—with your father in a delicate state at the hospital, and with your younger sister to care for—I think you should know what's happening here. I think you should know that I'm highly recommending your mother seek professional help."

"I don't understand." I did not want to understand.

"She's been cutting herself," he said sharply, angrily, as if he hated me for forcing him to say it out loud, to say it to a child. "She's self-harming. I think she needs to be in therapy."

He gave me something, a piece of paper with something written on it, and assured me there would be more information in her file, with the nurse, or someone, somewhere. He'd recommended a doctor, a program. Grief counseling.

"She's going to be okay," he said, clapping a hand on my shoulder. I nearly fell to the ground. "She just needs time. And she needs support."

I carried the tea tray into the living room with trembling hands, glass shuddering against metal, jangling against itself. My mother was smiling at something my sister was saying, her delicate hands clasped in her lap. She was a beautiful woman, lithe with big, dark eyes. Few others had the privilege of seeing her like this, her long hair curling around her shoulder in a single brown wave. She looked up as I entered. Smiled wider.

"Bea beshin, azizam." *Come sit down, my dear.*

She thanked me for making tea, thanked me when I poured her the cup, thanked me again when I handed it to her. She was trying too hard, and it was making my heart pound.

"I'm sorry I scared you," she said in Farsi, her eyes shining. She laughed, shook her head. "Anyway, khodaroshokr"—*thank God*—"everything is fine. The doctor said I just need to get more sleep. This tea is excellent, by the way."

It was not. I'd taken too long to bring it out, and the temperature of the tea had dropped just below what was acceptable, which was a tea so boiling hot it burned your throat. If my mother were herself she would've sent it back.

Even my sister seemed to realize that.

"The tea is cold," Shayda said, frowning.

This was a gross exaggeration. The tea was plenty hot, hot enough for any sane person. It just wasn't *boiling* hot.

"The tea is fine," my mother said, waving dismissively. She took a sip. She was still speaking in Farsi. "Your father is doing better, by the way. They think he might come home soon."

"What?" I blanched. I nearly dropped my cup. "But I thought they said his situation was critical. I thought—"

"You are unbelievable, Shadi."

I looked up, surprised, to meet my sister's eyes.

"You can't even hide your disappointment. What, were you *hoping* he'd die? What kind of a horrible person hopes for their father to die?"

I felt that familiar, stinging heat rise up my throat again, press against my teeth, sear the whites of my eyes.

The nurse found cuts on her wrists and on her legs, the doctor had said. *Some were relatively fresh. Has she ever said anything to make you think she might be a danger to herself?*

My mother shook her head. "Don't be ridiculous," she said in rapid-fire Farsi. "That's a slanderous thing to say about a person."

"And yet, she doesn't deny it's true."

My mother turned to me, eyes wide. "Shadi?"

Heat knotted together at the base of my throat. I shook my head, about to lie a perfect, beautiful lie when the doorbell rang.

I jumped to my feet.

I was happy for the interruption, but also, I was the only one among us still wearing a scarf. I touched my head absently, the wilted silk somehow still intact. I marveled at that, at how I'd forgotten to take it off. I'd forgotten to do all kinds of things. Forgotten to eat, for example. Or shower. I'd forgotten to bandage the cut on my knee, forgotten to wash the blood off my chin.

That was the first thing my mother said to me when she saw me, the first thing she did. She took my chin in her hand and yelled at me, demanded to know what I'd done to my face, as if my wound were greater than hers.

She doesn't know I'm telling you this, the doctor had said. *She begged me not to tell you or your sister.*

I swallowed against the rising heat, swallowed against the stinging burn. I moved toward the front door and heard the rain howl, lash against the windows. I reached for the handle just as my mother laughed, the soft trill wrenching apart my heart.

I opened the door.

For the second time today, someone stood before me and held aloft my ugly blue backpack. Ali's clothes were wet. His hair was soaked. His eyelashes were sooty, glittering with damp. In the warm glow of the porch light, I saw him as I hadn't earlier: hyperreal, many-dimensional. He was tall, even imposing, his skin a golden brown without blemish, the lines of his face sharp, beautiful. What was once a clean shave had given way to a 10 p.m. shadow, adding an unexpected depth to his appearance. He'd probably not looked in a mirror in hours. He probably had no idea what he looked like, no idea the picture he presented. A single drop of rain dripped down his forehead, slid along his nose, tucked itself between his lips. He prized them open.

"You forgot this in my car," he said quietly.

My eyes were filling with tears again, had been threatening to fill all night. I pushed back the army with almighty force, felt their fire travel down my esophagus, set my insides aflame.

"You okay?" Over and over again, he asked me this question. He was staring at me ruthlessly, his eyes lingering on my face, the cut on my chin. I felt the friction between us as palpably as I felt the pounding in my heart. He was angry. Afraid. He stared at me with an authority I found surprising, with a concern I'd not felt in a long time. I watched him swallow as he waited. His throat was wet; the movement was mesmerizing.

"Please," he whispered. "Please answer me."

I didn't lift my head.

"Are you okay?"

"No," I said, and took the bag.

I heard his exhale; it was a tortured sound. "Shadi—"

"Who is it?" my mom asked, her voice carrying over from the living room. "Is it a package?"

"Bye," I said softly, and closed the door in his face.

NINE

Were I a fly perched upside down, legs clinging to a fiber ceiling, I would've seen a sea of hairy heads bent over papers placed atop desks, human hands clenched around number two pencils, each seat showcasing a similar scene save one.

Mine.

My silk head turned in sharp, erratic movements, my mind unable to settle. I had an exam today in my AP Art History class, an exam for which I'd not had the opportunity to prepare. I fell asleep last night in molting silk, fully dressed and freezing, awoke in my own blood. The wound on my chin had ripped open as I slept and I found evidence of this fact on my pillow, in my hair, smeared across my eyelids. In my dreams my teeth rotted, fell out of my head, I screamed the screams of dreams that made no sound and sat straight up at the screech of my alarm, my chest tight with terror.

It seemed my constant companion, this feeling, this word. *Terror.*

It haunted me, tormented me, terror, terrifying, terrorist, terrorism, these were my definitions in the dictionary along with my face and surname, first name, date of birth.

I'd made more of an effort than usual this morning, convinced, somehow, that eyeliner would detract from the bandage on my chin. I didn't want the world to know my secrets, didn't want my wounds torn open before the masses, and yet, there was no escaping notice. I'd already had to listen to someone make a joke they thought I didn't hear, something low, a laugh, a tittering: "Looks like someone punched Osama in the face last night," followed by an "Oh my God, Josh, shut up," all neatly rounded out by another chorus of laughter. I was a turkey carved up every day, all manner of passersby eager for a piece. My flesh had been so thoroughly stripped I was now more bone than meat, with little left to give up but my marrow.

I stared at the printed sheet in front of me now, the ink swimming. My eyes felt perpetually hot, overheated, my heart poorly digested in my gut. I tapped my pencil on the page, stared at a block of text I was meant to analyze, a painting I was meant to recognize. For the third time in the last half hour, I felt a pair of eyes on my face.

This time, I did not pretend them away.

This time, I lifted my head, looked in their direction. The eyes quickly averted, the familiar face bowed once again over her paper, hand scribbling furiously at nonsense.

Due to the nature of the art history course—and the interminable amount of time we spent staring at slides—our class was held in the only amphitheater on campus. We were all arranged in an incomplete circle, our raised seats gradually descending toward a single podium in the middle of the room behind which was a massive screen. The teacher currently stood sentinel in the center, watching us closely as we worked. Our class didn't have assigned seats, but I always sat toward the back, where the desks were illuminated by only dim lighting, and when Zahra glanced my way for the fourth time, I marveled that she could see me at all.

Her attention toward me did not bode well.

I glanced at my exam again. Thirty minutes in, and I'd written only four things: my name, my class, the period number, and the date. My eyes homed in on the year.

2003.

I felt my mind spiral, rewind its own tape, a pencil in the cassette reel spinning backward. Memories surfaced and dissolved, sounds streaking into flashes of light. I conjured a vague, distorted impression of my slightly younger self, marveled at her naivete. Last year I had no idea the extent of what was coming for me. No idea, even now, how I would survive it.

My breath caught.

Pain speared me without warning, a javelin through the throat. I forced myself to take a calming breath, forced myself to return to the present moment, to the pressing task at hand.

We were down to twenty minutes in class and I hadn't yet answered a single question. I reached for my pencil, compelled myself to focus.

My fingers closed around air.

I frowned. Looked around. I was about to give up on the writing instrument I thought I'd had, about to reach into my bag for a new one when someone tapped me, gently, on the shoulder.

I turned.

Wordlessly, my neighbor handed over my pencil. "You dropped it," he mouthed.

I stared at him for just a moment too long, my mind catching up to my body as if on a delay.

My heart was pounding.

"Thank you," I finally said, but even my whisper was too loud. I ignored a few fleeting looks from my classmates, sat back in my seat. I glanced again at my neighbor out of the corner of my eye, though not surreptitiously enough. He met my gaze, smiled.

I averted my eyes, worried I'd just made myself seem more than casually interested in this guy. Noah. His name was Noah. He was one of the only Black kids in our school, which was enough to make him memorable, but more than that—he was new. He'd transferred in about a month ago, and I didn't think I'd ever spoken to him prior to this moment. In fact, I couldn't presently recall ever sitting next to him. Then again, there were forty-five students in this class, and I couldn't trust my memory; I was terrible at noticing details these days. Then again *again*, I didn't think I was so checked out that I couldn't even remember who sat next to me in class.

I slumped lower in my chair.

Concentrate.

The painting poorly printed on my exam came suddenly into sharp focus. Two women were working together to behead a man, one pinning him to the mattress as he struggled, the other sawing into his throat with a dagger. I tapped my pencil against the picture; my heart thudded nervously in my chest.

I closed my eyes for a second, two seconds, more.

Ali's reappearance last night had dredged up feelings I hadn't allowed myself to think about in months. I seldom allowed myself to think about last year, my junior year; I often thought it a miracle I was still alive to remember those days at all. September of last year my heart had been left for dead under an avalanche of emotion delivered in triplicate:

Love. Hate. Grief.

Three different blows delivered in quick succession. I was stunned to discover, all these months later, that hatred had been the hardest to overcome.

Artemisia Gentileschi.

Her name came to me all at once: Artemisia Gentileschi, one of the most critically acclaimed and simultaneously overlooked painters of the seventeenth century. My mind parroted back to me the information I'd once memorized, names and dates I'd made into flash cards. Born in Rome, 1593. Died in Naples, 1653.

I knew the answers, but my hand would not move. I felt my lungs constrict as panic flooded my chest. The tips of my fingers went numb, sparked back to life. I could hardly hold my pencil.

This painting can be attributed to a follower of Caravaggio based on which of the following formal qualities?
A) Monochromatic palette
B) Dramatic tenebrism
C) Pyramidal composition
D) Prominent grisaille

My relationship with Zahra had been strained for a while, but last September tensions between us reached their pinnacle, an achievement for which there seemed no obvious impetus. Still, I spent the last year of our friendship navigating a maze of passive aggression, parrying every day the thinly veiled insults she lobbed my way. It only occurred to me now that Zahra had held on to our friendship a year longer than she'd wanted. She'd not been so reprehensible a person to kick me while I was down; she had enough mercy, at least, to spare me such a blow so soon after my brother died.

I should've seen it coming.

I should've, but I'd been willfully blind. I'd been so mired in grief I could hardly survive my parents' nightly fights, could hardly survive the rigorous demands of my junior year. I was desperate for even the scraps of the familiar, desperate to hold on to the friend who knew my history, to the escape that was her home. I'd not been able to spare the emotional expense necessary to see what was right in front of me—that my best friend had begun to hate me.

Hate me.

When the bell rang, I turned in a blank exam.

LAST YEAR

PART III

PART III

My mom was waiting for me after school, her champagne-colored minivan wedged between two nearly identical models. I knew her minivan was a champagne color—not a variation on beige, not a sort-of-brown—but *champagne*, specifically, because the salesman who'd sold it to my parents had emphasized the color as a selling point.

My poor parents had been scandalized.

They'd sat the salesman down and explained to him that they did not drink alcohol, they did not want a *champagne* car, could they please have a different one.

I smiled now, remembering this story—Mehdi loved telling it at social gatherings—and trudged toward our drunken minivan, Zahra trailing behind. The after-school pickup was always a logistical nightmare, but my mom had long ago found a way to manage it: she arrived half an hour early, and usually she brought a book. Today, however, she was squinting through her reading glasses at the glossy pages of a magazine, a publication I wasn't immediately able to identify.

I rapped on the window when we arrived, and my mom jumped a foot in her seat. She turned and scowled at me, set down the magazine.

"Hi," I said, beaming at her.

My mom rolled her eyes, smiled. The side door slid open and we all exchanged hellos, settled into our seats. The minivan's interior smelled vaguely of Cheez-Its, which, for some reason, I found comforting.

My mom tugged off her reading glasses.

"Madreseh khoob bood?" *Was school okay?* Then, to Zahra: "Zahra joonam, chetori?" *Zahra dear, how are you?* "How's your mom?"

Zahra was busy responding to my mother in flawless Farsi when I noticed, with a start, the discarded magazine on the console.

I picked it up.

It was an old issue of *Cosmopolitan* featuring a highly airbrushed photo of Denise Richards—under whose name it read: *Be Naughty with Him!* And, as if that weren't alarming enough, there was the headline—in bold, white type—

Our Best Sex Secret

I looked up. Zahra was saying something to my mom about SAT prep courses, and I couldn't wait. I cut her off.

"Hey," I said, shaking the magazine at my mom. "Hey, what the hell is this?"

My mom stilled. She spared me a single glance before inserting the key in the ignition. "Man chemidoonam," she said. *How am I supposed to know?* "It was at the dentist's office."

Zahra laughed. "Um, Nasreen khanoom"—*Mrs. Nasreen*—"I don't think you're supposed to take the magazines."

"Eh? Vaughan?" My mom turned on the car. *Oh? Really?*

I was shaking my head. I did not believe for a second that my mom thought the old, grimy magazines at the dentist's office were free for the taking. "So is the secret any good?" I asked. "Because it says right here"—I scanned the cover again—"that it's *a secret so hot, so breathtaking, experts are raving about it.*"

My mom was driving now, but she still managed to glare at me in the rearview mirror. "Ay, beetarbiat." *Oh, you rude child.*

I was fighting back a smile. "Don't lie, Maman. I saw you reading it."

She said something in Farsi then, an expression difficult to translate. To put it simply: she threatened to kick my ass when we got home.

I couldn't stop laughing.

Zahra had swiped the magazine, and she was now scanning the article in question. Slowly, she looked up at me.

"Oh my God," she whispered. "I love your mom."

My mother muttered something like *What am I supposed to do with you kids?* in Farsi, and then turned on the radio.

My mom loved pop radio.

Currently, she was a loyal fan of Enrique Iglesias, because she grew up listening to his dad—Julio Iglesias—and when Enrique was first introduced on the radio she clasped her heart and sighed. These days she championed Enrique Iglesias as if it were her civic duty, as if Julio were watching and she hoped to make him proud. Right now, *Escape* was blasting through the speakers at a ridiculous volume, in what was no doubt an effort to drown out our voices.

"Hey," I shouted, "you're not getting off that easily."

"Chi?" she shouted back. *What?*

I tried for a higher decibel. "I said, *you're not getting off that easily.*"

"What?" She cupped a hand to her ear, pretended to be deaf.

I fought back another laugh and shook my head at her. She smiled, put on her sunglasses, adjusted her scarf, and gently bobbed her head to the music.

"Hey." Zahra tapped my knee. "Shadi?"

I turned, raised my eyebrows. "Yeah?"

"We're, like, five minutes away from my house," she said, glancing out the window. "And I just—before I go, I wanted to say sorry. Again. About today."

"Oh," I said, surprised. "It's okay."

"It's not okay. I shouldn't have just attacked you like that." She sat back in her seat, stared into her hands. "Ali just— He always gets everything, you know? Things are so easy for him. Relationships. Friendships. He doesn't know what it's like for me, what it's like to wear hijab or how horrible people can be or how hard it is to make friends."

"I know," I said softly. "I know."

"I know you do." She smiled then, her eyes shining with feeling. "You're like the only one who gets it. And everything is just"—she shook her head, looked out the window—"school is so fucking brutal right now. Do you remember that guy who pulled off my scarf?"

I stiffened. "Of course."

"He keeps following me around," she said, swallowing. "And it's really freaking me out."

I felt my chest constrict with panic and I fought it back, kept my face placid for her sake. "Why didn't you tell me?"

"I don't know. I thought maybe I was imagining things."

"We'll report him," I said sharply. "We'll tell someone."

Zahra laughed. "As if that'll make any difference."

"Hey"—I took her hands, squeezed—"look, I'll stay with you. I'll walk you to class. I'll make sure you're not alone."

She took a deep breath, her chest shuddering as she exhaled. "This is stupid, Shadi. This whole situation is so stupid. Why do we even have to have these conversations? Why do I have to be scared all the time? Why? Because of a bunch of ignorant assholes?"

"I know. I know, I hate it, too."

She shook her head, shook off the emotion. "I'm just—I'm sorry I'm taking things out on you. I don't mean to."

"I know."

"Everyone is different now. All my old friends. Even some of the teachers." She looked away. "I think I'm worried I'm going to lose you, too."

"You're not going to lose me."

"I know." She laughed, wiped her eyes. "I know. I'm sorry. I know." But when she looked up again, she looked uncertain. She whispered: "So you're really not hooking up with my brother?"

"Zahra." I sighed. Shook my head. "Come on."

"I'm sorry, I know, I'm crazy." She squeezed her eyes shut. "I just—I don't know. Sometimes I need to hear you say it."

I stole a furtive glance at my mom, who was now tapping the steering wheel along to a Nelly song.

"Zahra," I said sharply. "I am not hooking up with your brother."

She smiled at that, seemed suddenly delighted. "And you're not going to, like, fall in love with him and ditch me?"

I rolled my eyes. "No. I am not going to fall in love with him and ditch you."

"You promise?"

"Wow, okay, now you're starting to piss me off."

She laughed.

I laughed.

And just like that, I had my best friend back.

DECEMBER

2003

TEN

I left the classroom with the tide, grateful today, as I was most days, that our school was home to the nearly three thousand students who gave me the cover to disappear. I felt lucky, too, that our student body included just enough Muslim kids— and a couple of girls who wore hijab—that I didn't have to bear the weight of representation entirely on my own. Recently they'd formed a Muslim Student Union, an on-campus club through which they set up conferences and organized interfaith dialogues and patiently answered all manner of ignorant questions for the masses. The MSU president flagged me down a few times, generously inviting me to their events, and I never had the heart to say no to her. Instead, I'd do the more detestable thing, and make promises I never intended to keep. I avoided those kids not because I didn't admire them, but because I was a husk of a person with little fight left to give, and I didn't think they'd understand. Or maybe I was afraid they would.

Maybe I wasn't ready to talk.

In the two months since Zahra and I had parted ways, I'd been eating lunch alone. I was too tired to drum up the enthusiasm needed to strike up conversations with people who didn't know the intimate details of my life. I chose instead to sit far from the crowds, alone with my optimistic thoughts and my optimistic newspaper. Only recently had my innumerable attractions lured a stranger to my lunch table: a foreign exchange student from Japan who smiled often and said little. Her name was Yumiko. We were perfect for each other.

Dramatic tenebrism.

It hit me suddenly, like a slap to the head. The answer was *B. Dramatic tenebrism.* A less intense chiaroscuro.

Damn.

I sighed as I followed the sea of students down the hall. I had one more class before lunch, and I needed to switch out my books. Miraculously, my body knew this without prompting; the autopilot feature had flickered on in my brain and was already guiding my feet down a familiar path to my locker. I pushed my way through a tangle of bodies, found the metal casket that housed my things, spun the dial on the lock. My hands moved mechanically, swapping textbooks for textbooks, my eyes seeing nothing.

It took very little for Zahra to ambush me.

I turned around and there she was, brown curls and

almond eyes, perfectly manicured brows furrowed, arms crossed at her chest.

She was angry.

I took a step back, felt the sharp edge of my open locker dig into my spine. It was all in my head, I knew that even then, but it seemed to me that the world stopped in that moment, the din dimmed, the light changed, a camera lens focused. I held my breath and waited for something, hoped for something, feared so much.

When Zahra first cut me out of her life, I had no idea what was happening. I didn't understand why she'd stopped eating lunch with me, didn't understand why she'd stopped returning my calls. She plucked me from her tree of life with such efficiency I didn't even realize what happened until I hit the ground.

After that, I let her go.

I made no demands, insisted on no explanations. Once I understood that she'd ejected me without so much as a goodbye, I'd not possessed the self-hatred necessary to beg her to stick around. Instead, I grieved quietly—in the privacy of my bedroom, on the shower floor, in the middle of the night. I'd learned from my mother to hide the pain that mattered most, to allow it an audience only behind closed doors, with only God as my witness. I had other friends, I knew other people. I was not desperate for company.

Still, I had violent dreams about her. I screamed at her in my delirium, sobbed while she stood over me and stared, her face impassive. I asked her questions she'd never answer, threw punches that never landed.

It felt strange to look at her now.

"Hi," I said quietly.

Her eyes flashed. "I want you to stop talking to my brother."

A cold weight drove into my chest, punctured a vital organ. "What?"

"I don't know what you're thinking or why you would even think it, but you have to stop throwing yourself at him. Stay away from him, stay away from me, and stay the hell out of my life—"

"Zahra, stop," I said sharply. "*Stop.*" My heart was racing so fast I felt it pounding in my head. "I'm not talking to your brother. I saw him yesterday by accident, and he drove me t—"

"By accident."

"Yes."

"You saw him by accident."

"Yes, I—"

"So you saw him by accident, he gave you a ride home by accident, you left your backpack in his car by accident, you were wearing his sweatshirt by *accident.*"

I drew in a sharp breath.

Something flickered in Zahra's eyes, something akin to triumph, and my composure broke. Anger filled my head with stunning speed, black heat edging into my vision. Through nothing short of a miracle, I fought it back.

"I've told you a hundred times," I said, "that I didn't know it was his. I thought that sweatshirt belonged to Mehdi. And I don't know why you refuse to believe me."

She shook her head, disgust marring the face that was once so familiar to me. "You're a shitty liar, Shadi."

"I'm not lying."

She wasn't listening. "Every time I asked if something was going on between you and my brother, you'd always act so innocent and hurt, like you had no idea what I was talking about. I can't believe you really thought I was that stupid. I can't believe you thought I wouldn't figure it out."

"Figure what out? What are you talking about?"

"Ali," she said angrily. "My brother. Did you think I wouldn't put it all together? Did you think I wouldn't notice what you did to him? God, if you were going to mess around with my brother the least you could've done was not break his fucking heart."

"What?" I was panicking. I could feel myself panicking. "Is that what he told you? Did he tell you that?"

"He didn't have to tell me. It was pretty easy to put the whole thing together." She made a gesture with her hand. "One day he comes home looking like he got shot in the chest, and the next day he stops speaking to you forever."

"No." I was shaking my head, shaking it so hard I felt dizzy. "No, that's not what happened. You don't unders—"

"*Bullshit*, Shadi." Her eyes were bright with an anger that scared me, worried me. I took an involuntary step back, but she followed.

"You lied to me for years. Not only did you hook up with my brother behind my back, but you broke his heart, and worst of all—God, Shadi, worst of all, you pretended to be so perfect and good, when that whole time you were actually just a slutty, lying piece of shit."

I felt, suddenly, like I'd gone numb.

"I just wanted you to know," she was saying. "I wanted you to know that I know the truth. Maybe no one else sees through all your bullshit—maybe everyone at the mosque thinks you're some kind of a saint—but I know better. So stay the hell away from my family," she said.

And walked away.

I stood there, staring into space until the final bell rang, until the chaotic hall became a ghost town. I was going to be late to my next class. I squeezed my eyes shut, tried to breathe.

I wanted, desperately, to disappear.

Zahra and I had been friends since I was eleven; I met her and Ali at the same time. Our family was new in town and my parents wanted us to make friends, so they sent me and Shayda and Mehdi to a Muslim summer camp, a camp none of us had wanted to attend. It was our shared loathing of spending summer afternoons listening to religious sermons that brought us all together. If only I'd known then that we'd usher in our end with a similar emotion.

Zahra had always hated me, just a little bit.

She'd always said it like it was a joke, a charming turn of phrase, like it was normal to roll your eyes and say every other day, *God, I hate you so much*, to the person who was, ostensibly, your best friend. For years, her hatred was innocuous enough to ignore—she hated the way I avoided coffee, hated how I took the evil eye seriously, hated the sad music I listened to, hated the way I turned into a prim, obedient child when I spoke Farsi—but in the last year, her hatred had changed.

I think, deep down, I'd always known we wouldn't last.

I'd known about Zahra's old pain; I knew she'd been used and discarded by other girls who'd feigned interest in her friendship only to get close to her brother. I tried always to be sensitive to this, to make sure she knew that our friendship was more important to me than anything. What I hadn't realized was how paranoid she'd become over the years, how she'd already painted upon my face a picture of her own insecurities. She was so certain that I'd ditch her for Ali that she nearly fulfilled her own prophecy just to be right, just to prove to me—and to herself—that I'd been worthless all along.

Soon, she hated everything about me.

She hated how much her parents liked me, hated how they were always inviting me to things. But most of all, she hated, *hated*, that I was always asking to come over to her house.

I felt a flush of heat move across my skin at the memories, ancient mortification refusing to die.

I just want to know why, okay? Why do you always want to come over? Why are you always here? Why do you always want to spend the night? Why?

I'd told her the truth a thousand times, but she never

believed me for longer than a week before she was suspicious again. And so it went, my screams soldiering on in their usual vein, unnoticed.

ELEVEN

I dropped my backpack on the damp, pebbled concrete, took a seat on the dirty curb. I stared out at the sea of glistening cars quietly settling in the parking lot of an outdoor shopping mall.

So this was freedom.

Yumiko and I had spent enough lunches together now that I'd begun to feel a sense of obligation toward our meetings. I always tried to tell her when I wouldn't be around, and though I'd invited her to join me on this unexciting sojourn off campus, she gently reminded me that she was only a junior. Seniors alone were allowed to leave school for lunch, but given the time restraints—and my lack of a car—the local shopping mall was as far as I ever got, which often diminished my motivation to make the effort.

Today, however, I'd needed the walk.

I'd purchased a slice of pizza from a beloved local place, a place run by a guy named Giovanni. Giovanni was never able to hide his disappointment when I showed up. Giovanni always broke into a sweat when I walked in, his eyes darting around nervously as I ordered. Giovanni and I both knew his real name was Javad, and he'd never forgiven me for asking him, out loud, in front of a long line of people, whether he was Iranian.

When he'd denied it, looking aghast at the insinuation, I was dumbstruck. I'd stared at the crayon drawings taped to the wall behind his head, shakily done stick figures with titles like *baba* and *amoo*.

Dad. Uncle.

I hadn't known it was a secret. His Iranian accent was so thick I was astonished anyone was dumb enough to accept it as Italian. And I'd heard such great things about Giovanni's that, when I first showed up and discovered a Persian man behind the counter, I was delighted. Proud.

Javad never looked me in the eye anymore.

I bit into my cold slice of pizza, retrieved the newspaper from my waistband. I cracked the paper open with one hand, took a second bite of pizza with the other. I felt a familiar dread as I scanned the headlines, and prepared for a deep dive into a brand-new existential crisis.

"Hey." A body collapsed beside me with an exhale, blocked my view of a particularly dirty minivan. "Okay if I sit here?"

I stared, unblinking, at the newcomer.

To say that I was confused would've been a disservice to the maelstrom of thoughts suddenly kicked up in my head.

Noah from AP Art History was sitting next to me, and I gaped at him like he'd opened a third eye. I'd forgotten my manners entirely.

Noah's smile faded.

He picked up his plate, the paper graying with pizza grease. "I can go," he said, moving to stand. "I didn't mean t—"

"No. Oh my God. No, of course you can stay," I said too quickly, too loudly. "Please stay. I was just—surprised."

His smile grew back, bigger this time. "Cool."

I attempted a smile of my own before picking up my newspaper again. I shook out the crease, tried to find my spot. I didn't mind Noah sitting next to me, not as long as he was willing to be quiet. I'd never had a chance to finish reading a piece about the terrifying similarities between the Iraq and Vietnam Wars, and I'd been waiting all day to get back to it. I took another bite of pizza.

"So, um, your name is Shadi, right?"

I looked up. Felt the distant world come back into focus.

I saw only Noah's eyes over the top of my paper, and I realized then that I'd never studied him closely. I folded the paper down; the rest of his face came into view. His black curls were cropped close to his head, his deep-set eyes a couple shades darker than his brown skin. He had unusually striking features—something about his cheekbones, the line of his nose. He was undeniably good-looking. I didn't know why he was talking to me.

"Yes." I frowned. "You're Noah?"

"Yeah." His eyes lit up. He seemed delighted by this, the revelation that I knew his name. "I just moved here. Like, last month."

"Oh. Wow." I gestured with my pizza to the damp, depressing parking lot. "I'm sorry."

He laughed. "It's not so bad."

I raised an eyebrow.

He bit back another laugh. "Yeah, okay. It's pretty bad."

I cracked a smile then. Picked up my paper.

"So, um, you're Muslim, right?"

I was still reading when I said, "What gave it away?"

He laughed for a third time. I liked that he laughed so much, so easily. The sound alone made my heart kick a little.

"Yes," I said, my face buried in the article. "I'm Muslim."

Gently, he pushed the newspaper down, away from me, and I flinched at his closeness, sat back an inch. He was staring at me with barely suppressed mirth, like he was fighting a smile.

"What?"

"Okay," he said finally. "Okay. I'm going to say something right now, and please don't take this the wrong way or anything"—he held up his hands—"but I didn't think you'd be so funny."

I raised both eyebrows. *"Don't take this the wrong way?"*

"You just seem so intense all the time," he said, his whole body like an exclamation point. "Like, why are you always reading the newspaper? That seems unhealthy."

I frowned at him. "I'm a masochist."

He frowned back. "Doesn't that mean you like to hurt people?"

"It means I like to hurt myself."

"Weird."

"Hey, how do you know I'm always reading the newspaper?"

Noah's smile slipped. He looked suddenly nervous. "Okay—please don't freak out—"

"Jesus Christ, Noah."

"Wait—are you talking to me?" He pointed at himself. "Or are you just listing prophets?"

My eyes widened.

He couldn't stop laughing, not even when he said, "Okay, okay, complete honesty: I've been, like, trying to figure out how to talk to you for a little while."

I sighed. Put down the paper. "Let me guess: you're a serial killer."

"I'm not! I swear, I just—I promised to do my mom a favor, and I didn't know exactly how to approach you."

I straightened. Noah suddenly had my full attention; I was one hundred percent freaked out. "What kind of favor?"

"Nothing weird."

"*Oh my God.*"

He spoke in a rush. "Okay, so, my mom was dropping me off at school one day and she saw you on campus and she wanted me to talk to you."

"Why?" I was suddenly wishing I'd never gone out for lunch. I was suddenly wishing I'd told Noah not to sit next to me.

He sighed. "Because we're new here, and my parents have been looking for a mosque to go to, and my mom thought you'd—"

"Wait." I held up a hand, cut him off. "You're Muslim?"

He frowned. "Did I not mention that?"

I hit him with my newspaper. "What the hell is wrong with you? You scared the crap out of me."

"I'm sorry!" He jerked out of reach. "I'm sorry. My mom just saw a girl in hijab and sent me on a mission to talk to you like it was normal, and it's not normal. It's super awkward."

I shot him a look. "More awkward than *this*?"

"You're right. I'm sorry." But his attempt at penitence was belied by his smile. "So? Can you help me out?"

I sighed. "Yes."

"Cool."

"But I swear to God," I said, narrowing my eyes at him, "if you turn out to be an undercover FBI agent I will be so pissed."

"What?" His smile vanished. "FBI agent?"

My guilt was instantaneous.

Noah looked suddenly freaked out, so different from his lighthearted mien a moment ago, and I didn't like that I'd put that look on his face. His family had just moved here; I didn't want to scare him.

"Nothing." I forced a smile. "I was just giving you a hard time."

"Oh," he said. "Okay." But the wariness in his eyes said he wasn't sure if he believed me.

I tried to move past it.

"So, there are a couple of different mosques around here," I explained, "but the one my family goes to has a predominantly Persian congregation. I can give you other—"

"Oh, no, that's perfect." Noah's smile returned in full force. "My mom will love that. I'm half-Persian."

I went suddenly stupid. I stared at him, slack-jawed. "What?"

He was laughing again. "Damn, the look on your face right now. I wish you could see yourself."

"You're half-Persian?"

"I speak a little Farsi, too." He cleared his throat, made a big show. "*Haleh shoma chetoreh?*"

"That's not terrible," I said, trying not to laugh. "So—your mom is Persian?"

He nodded. "Yeah."

"That's so cool. That makes me so happy."

He raised an eyebrow. "Why happy?"

"I don't know." I hesitated. "I guess I thought most Persian people were racist."

Noah froze, his eyes widening. Then he laughed so hard he doubled over. He laughed so hard it attracted notice, passersby pausing to stare at the source of the unbridled sound.

"Hey. Stop." I pushed at his arm to get his attention. "Why are you laughing?"

He shook his head, wiped tears from his eyes. "I'm just—" He shrugged, shook his head again, his shoulders still shaking with silent laughter. "Just, damn, Shadi. Wow."

"*What?*"

"I'm just glad you said it and not me." He took a sharp breath, held it, let it go as he stared into the distance. "Man, my mom is going to love that. You don't even know the shit my parents have had to deal with."

"I can only imagine."

"Well, you'd be the first to try. People never want to admit we have problems like that in our own communities." He sighed, shook his head, jumped to his feet. "All right, we should go. We're going to be late."

I realized then that I didn't even know what time it was. It had been too long since I'd spent my lunch break focused on anything but the fractures in my heart, and when I got to my feet, I felt a little lighter.

Noah and I tossed our plates, walked back to campus. I told him the name of our mosque. Gave him a phone number his mom could call. We were nearly back at school when I remembered—

"Oh, hey, I'll be there this weekend, actually. My sister and I volunteer on Saturday nights to help people learn how to use computers, set up email addresses, that sort of thing. If your parents want to stop by, I can introduce them to some people."

Noah raised his eyebrows. "Saturday night computer classes at the mosque. Nice."

My smiles were coming more easily now. "We have a lot of refugees in our community," I explained. "People who fled

Afghanistan, ran for their lives from the Taliban. There are a few people at our mosque whose entire families were beheaded by Saddam Hussein. Most of them came here with nothing, and they need help getting started again."

"Jesus," he said, sobering quickly.

"Yeah," I said. "Their stories are insane."

"Insane how?"

A sharp breeze stole into my jacket then, and I struggled, for a moment, to pull the zipper closed.

"I don't know," I said, shoving my hands in my pockets. "Like, you know what a burqa is? Those gross tent things the Taliban forces women to wear in Afghanistan?"

He nodded.

"Well, apparently they're really good for hiding people. Imagine disguising your entire family—men, women, children—in those burqas, and running for your life through the mountains and deserts of Afghanistan, hoping at every turn not to be found out and executed."

"Holy shit." We'd come to an abrupt stop at an intersection. Noah turned to look at me, his eyes wide. "You actually know people who did that? Went through that?"

"Yeah," I said, hitting the button for the crosswalk. "They go to our mosque."

"That's . . . crazy."

Noah's solemn tone—and his proceeding silence—made me aware, a beat too late, of the dark tension I'd just carried into the conversation. We were still waiting at the crosswalk, quietly watching the seconds tick down until the light would change.

I tried to salvage the moment.

"Hey," I said, pasting a smile on my face, "you're welcome to join us on Saturday night. We might even order pizza."

Noah laughed, raised his eyebrows at me. "That's quite an offer."

"It's also worth noting," I said, "that it will be extremely boring."

"Amazing." He shook his head slowly, his smile growing impossibly wider. "I mean, I'm going to pass? But thanks."

"Honestly, if you'd said yes I would've judged you."

He laughed.

Noah and I had classes in different directions, so we split up when we got back to the campus parking lot. He was already several feet away when he turned back and shouted, "Hey, I'll find you at lunch tomorrow." He pointed at me. "I'll even bring my own newspaper."

I was still smiling long after he disappeared from sight.

I felt strangely buoyant, more like a real person than I'd felt in a long time. I tried to hold on to the feeling as I wended my way through the parked vehicles, but my luck abruptly ran out.

It was moments like this that made me believe in fate.

It seemed impossible that coincidence alone could account for the thousand tiny decisions I'd made today that nudged my feet into this exact position, at precisely this hour, into the wrong person at the wrong time. Everything around me seemed suddenly to be happening in slow motion, the scene pulling apart to make room for my thoughts, my unprocessed emotions. And then, all at once, the moment hurled itself back together with a gasp.

Mine.

My breath left my body in a single, painful exhalation as my back slammed into metal, my head spinning.

A girl was standing in front of me. My ears were still ringing from the impact, from the severe turn my body had to make in order to now be flattened against a parked vehicle. I counted four heads—three girls, one guy. The one who shoved me had long, dirty-blond hair that moved when she did, and I was staring at those limp yellow waves when she stabbed me in the collarbone with a single finger, her face contorting as she shouted.

I felt my mind dissolve.

My brain retreated from my body, panic shutting down my nervous system. Everything seemed to disconnect inside of my skull. I heard her words as if from a distance, as if I were someone else watching this happen to someone else. I listened as she told me to go back to where I came from, listened as she called me a filthy towelhead, stared at her as she stared at me, her eyes bright with a violence I found breathtaking.

And then, suddenly, she stopped.

She was done, all done, just a couple of angry sentences and that was it, the moment was over. I frowned. I'd thought, for some reason, that there'd be more, something new. I'd been stopped at least a dozen times by people who'd all spoken these exact same lines to me, and I was beginning to realize that none of them talked to each other, compared notes, jazzed things up.

She jerked back, let me go.

I straightened too quickly, nearly stumbled. Blood rushed back into my head, my nerves fired back to life. Sounds seemed suddenly too loud, the ground too far. My heartbeat was strange.

The girl was frowning at me.

She was frowning at me like she was confused, maybe disappointed. And then—so suddenly I could practically see the moment she answered her own question—her eyes lit up.

"Oh my God, you don't even speak English, do you?" She started laughing. "Oh my God, you don't even fucking speak English."

She laughed again and again, hysterically now, a hyena. "This fucking piece of shit doesn't even fucking speak English," she said to the sky, to the moon, to her friends, and they laughed and laughed and laughed.

This wasn't new, either.

People always assumed I wasn't born here. They always assumed I wasn't American, that English wasn't my first language.

People, I knew, thought I was dumb.

I didn't care.

I closed my eyes, let the pain leak from my body. I waited for them to get tired of me, waited for them to leave. I waited, quietly, because there was nothing else I could do.

I'd promised my mom I'd never engage with bigots, never talk back, never make a scene. Shayda had refused to make such promises to my mother, so my mom had turned to me instead, begging me to be reasonable, to walk away, to exercise the self-restraint that Shayda refused to employ. So I'd promised. Sworn it. I took the hits to my pride for my mother, for my mother alone. She was the reason I seldom spoke these days, the reason I didn't fight.

My mother.

And the police, if I'm being honest. The police and the FBI. The CIA. DHS. The Patriot Act. Guantanamo Bay. The No Fly List.

When I opened my eyes again, the group was gone.

I collected myself, gathered my bones. I walked to class on unsteady legs, clenched and unclenched my shaking hands. I felt my heart grow harder as I moved through the halls, felt it get heavier.

One day, I worried, it would simply fall out.

TWELVE

I sat in the wet grass after school, pulled my knees up to my injured chin. I was perilously close to something that felt like a flood, oceans dammed behind my eyes. I did not hope for a ride home today; I was merely tired. My father had been unable to work for nearly a month now, and my mom had taken a part-time job at Macy's to help with the pressure on our finances, which meant that my sister's mercy was the axis upon which my world turned—which meant my world was oft static, merciless.

I lifted my head, took a deep breath, drew the scent of cold wind and wet dirt into my body.

Petrichor.

It was a strange word, an excellent word.

You know there's a word for that, right? Ali had said to me once. *For that smell. The smell of water hitting the earth.*

I'd been standing in the backyard of my old house breathing in the drizzle when Ali said those words, walking toward me in the dark. Our living room had a sliding glass door that opened to the yard, and he'd left it open in his wake; I'd looked past him, past his milky, silhouetted stride to the glow of bodies in the living room, all of them laughing, talking. Remnants of conversation carried over to us in the darkness, and the effect was unexpectedly cozy. Ali's family had come over for dinner, but I'd disappeared after dessert, wanting to escape the commotion for a moment with the evening breeze.

"You left the door open," I'd said. "All the bugs are going to get inside."

He'd smiled. "It's called petrichor."

I shook my head, smiled back. "I know what it's called."

"Right." He laughed. Looked up at the sky. "Of course you do."

"Ali, the mosquitoes are going to eat everyone alive."

He glanced back. "Someone will close the door."

I'd rolled my eyes at him, started heading for the house. "They're not going to notice until it's—"

I jumped back, suddenly, when my foot sank into a muddy patch of grass, and promptly collided into Ali, who'd been following me inside. I'd been wearing a silk dress that summer day, but when he touched me, I might've been wearing nothing at all. The delicate fabric did little to dull the blow of sensation; I felt his hands on me like they were pressed against my skin, like I was naked in his arms.

I'd felt it, too, when he became aware of me, of the shape of me under his hands. When we collided he'd caught me from behind; I couldn't see his face. Instead, I'd felt his weight pressed up against my own, heard the change in his breath when we touched, when his hands froze where they'd landed. One of his palms was flat against my stomach, the other holding fast to my hip. He let go of me slowly, with excruciating care, like he'd caught a crystal bowl in midair. His fingers grazed my torso as they retreated, skated across my belly button. We'd both gone quiet, the sounds of our breathing amplified in the silence.

Ali had finally drawn back but I felt the whisper of his touch at the base of my spine, felt his chest move as he inhaled, exhaled. Softly—so softly it was little more than an idea—his fingers traced the indentation at my waist, the curve of my hips. He said, "God, Shadi, you're so beautiful sometimes I can't even look at you," and I'd just stood there, my heart jackhammering in my chest, my eyes closing on a sound, a desperate sound that escaped my lips, shattered the dream. I'd come back to myself with a terrifying awareness, walked back into the house without a word, without looking back.

Ali and I never discussed that moment, never even alluded to it. I think maybe we both knew, even then, that it was the beginning of something—something that might tear our lives to shreds.

I squeezed my eyes shut against the memory, pressed my forehead to my knees. Seeing Ali yesterday had broken the barricade in my mind meant to hold back precisely this kind of emotional stampede.

I needed to pull myself together.

I lifted my head, shoved my hands in my coat pockets, let the weather push me around. It wasn't raining, not yet, but it had been storming all day, crows circling, trees rattling. I loved watching things breathe, loved watching branches sway, leaves hanging on for dear life. I didn't mind the terrible gusts that nearly knocked back my scarf. There was something brutal about the wind, the way it slapped you in the face, left your ears ringing.

It made me feel alive.

The winds were currently too strong to allow a comfortable perusal of the newspaper, but there was a single cigarette abandoned in the linty lining of my right pocket, and I rolled it between my fingers, clenched and unclenched it in my fist. I nearly smiled.

These cigarettes had belonged to my brother.

I confiscated them before they came for his things, stole them out of their hiding places along with his weed, his dirty magazines, a box of condoms, and a single glass pipe. I didn't want him to do anything more to break my parents' hearts from beyond the grave. I didn't want him to be defined by his weaknesses any more than I wanted to be defined by mine. It seemed a terrible injustice to be exposed in death, to be found out as predictably human, as frail as everyone else.

My father knew, of course. Or at least suspected.

My father was a connoisseur of all things—he had, in fact, given this mantle to himself. He loved to hear himself speak aloud the truths he'd decided were holy, and he felt strongly about all manner of diverse subjects: worthy hobbies, the best attributes, a precise work ethic, the exact ratio of water to espresso in an Americano. He had many ideas about the world, ideas he'd spent his entire life honing, and which he often felt compelled to share, loudly, with the still-forming clay of his children. My dad often declared that he and my mother were decent, pious people who'd brought their children up to be better than drug addicts. Those were his words, my father's words, the ones he'd shouted when my brother came home with bloodshot eyes, smelling vaguely of weed for the umpteenth time.

My brother was a lazy liar.

Mehdi, too, drove a Honda Civic. A Honda Civic SI, bright blue, eighteen-inch rims. He'd modified it himself, put in a special exhaust, illegal blue lights, an insane sound system, a garish lip kit. He was expressly forbidden from drinking the alcohol he drank, expressly forbidden from dating the girls he dated, expressly forbidden from sneaking out of the house at night, which he did, nearly all the time. It was my window he used to climb out of, mine because of the ledge, the tree, the easy drop to the ground and the distance from my parents' bedroom. He'd always kiss me on the forehead before he left, and I'd always leave my phone under my pillow, waiting, waiting for the buzz of his late-night text message asking me to unlock the front door.

My father had never been cruel, but he had always been cold. He loved rules, and he demanded respect from his children. He no doubt thought he was doing the right thing by trying to control Mehdi, but my dad had been so focused on the differences between them that he never seemed to understand that they were also the same.

Unyielding.

My father tried to break him, so my brother became water. My father tried to contain him, so my brother became the sea.

I heard a sudden crash.

I got to my feet in time to see two cars collide, slide, spin wildly out of control. Screeching tires, the horrifying sound of metal devouring metal, glass shattering. Old panic rose up inside of me, stole my breath. I was running before I understood why, tearing across the grass in a frenzy. I fumbled for my phone and realized I didn't know where mine was, didn't remember what I'd done with it, didn't know where I'd left—

"*Call 911!*" I screamed at someone, my lungs on fire.

I was sprinting, realizing too late that I was still wearing this terrible backpack, deadweight dragging me down, and yet, for some reason, it didn't occur to me to drop it, to throw it aside. The asphalt was slick underfoot, some parts of the road flooded, and I barreled through the shallow rivers, not even feeling the icy water penetrate my skin. My heart thundered in my chest as I approached the wreckage, my emotions spiraling dangerously. I was only vaguely aware of myself, only vaguely aware that I might be overreacting, that perhaps I was the wrong person for this job, that perhaps there was an adult or a doctor around who could do better, be better, but somehow I couldn't stop, didn't know how.

One of the cars was discernibly worse off than the other and I headed there first, yanking on the damaged driver's side door until it opened with a miraculous groan. Inside, the driver was unconscious, her head bowed just above the steering wheel, a single line of blood trickling down her face.

Please, God, I thought. *Please, please.*

I reached around her, registering dimly that the airbags had not deployed, and tried to unbuckle her seat belt. It wouldn't unlatch. I yanked at it desperately, tried to rip the thing out from its base, but it wouldn't yield.

I heard the distant sound of sirens.

I yanked again at the seat belt, and this time, the girl stirred. She lifted her head with pronounced slowness, bleary eyes blinking open. She was maybe my age, just a kid, another kid, just a kid.

"Are you okay?" The scream of my voice startled me. "Are you all right?"

She frowned, looked around, realization dawning by painful degrees. I watched as her confusion gave way to understanding, understanding quickly giving way to a fear so profound it sent renewed horror through my body.

"Are you okay?" I said again, still hysterical. "Can you feel your legs? Do you know your name?"

"Oh my God," she said, and clapped her hands over

her mouth. "Oh my God, oh my God, ohmygodohmygod ohmygod—"

"What is it? What's wrong? The ambulance is almost here, someone called 911, don't—"

"My parents," she said, dropping her hands. Her face had paled. Her body had begun to tremble. "I just got my license. I'm not on the insurance yet. My parents are going to *kill* me, oh my God."

Something broke in me then, broke me down. I began shaking uncontrollably, my bones like dice in a closed fist. I sagged to the ground, knees digging into the wet, gritty asphalt. "Your parents," I said, gasping the words, "will be h-happy. So happy you're a-alive."

THIRTEEN

I heard shouting, deafening sirens, heavy, running footfalls. I dragged myself out of the way, staggered upright, headed for the sidewalk. I'd neither seen anything useful nor had I done anything of value; I did not need to leave behind my residue on the wreckage.

Besides, I hated talking to the police.

I made it to the sidewalk and stared at my feet, my heart beating erratically in my chest. I'd been fighting tears all day, all week, all year; it was exhausting. I often promised myself I'd cry them free when I got home, that I'd find a safe place to experience my anguish in full, and yet, I seldom did. It was not an exciting extracurricular activity, not the sort of thing most kids looked forward to upon arriving home from school. So I held them in. They remained here, unshed and overfilling my chest, pressing painfully against my sternum. Always threatening.

I looked up at the gray sky, watched a bird until I was thinking of birds, thought of birds until I was thinking of flight, thought of flight until I saw a plane, watched the plane until it soared away, left me behind.

Changed the subject.

A gale of wind tore past me and I stumbled, heard the trees shudder in the distance. The clouds were fattening, the birds were feverish. I didn't feel at all like myself but I was at least upright, nearly walking, so I figured I should continue on in this vein, trudge home, try to make it back before the rain knocked me sideways.

I'd only managed a few feet before I heard someone call my name.

Shout it, scream it.

I turned around, slightly stunned, and saw Ali standing not fifty feet away, planted in the middle of the sidewalk. His appearance alone was surprising enough, but what I couldn't understand was his face. Even from here, I could tell he was livid.

Fight or flight? Fight or flight?

I made no decision and instead waited for him to stalk over to me, his anger appearing to grow exponentially with every footfall. He wasn't quite ten feet away when he started yelling again, gesticulating at nothing when he said, "What the hell were you doing? What were you thinking?"

I frowned. I opened my mouth to protest my confusion but he was nearly upon me now, a footstep or two away from walking straight through me, and I wondered whether he would stop.

"Why would you run into the middle of a car accident?" he shouted. "You're not a paramedic. You're not trained for that. This isn't some kind of—" He stopped short suddenly, his words dying in his mouth.

"Jesus. I'm sorry. Don't cry. I'm sorry." He ran a hand through his hair, seemed agitated to an unnecessary degree. "I didn't mean to yell at you."

I hadn't realized I was crying. Horrified, I turned around, walked away, wiped at my cheeks with trembling hands.

"Wait—where are you going?" he said, keeping up.

I was still moving, now staring at a distant stoplight. I waited for the red light to turn green, waited for my body to stop shaking before I said, as steadily as I could manage, "What are you doing here?"

"What do you mean? I was picking my sister up from school."

I stopped walking.

In the last year of my friendship with Zahra, Ali refused to drive his sister to school, refused to pick her up. I thought I knew why—it seemed obvious he was trying to avoid me—and my hypotheses were occasionally validated by Zahra's mom, who'd suddenly become my only ride to and from school. It was a lot of work for Zahra's mom to shuttle us around everywhere, and she'd been looking forward to bullying Ali into doing some of the work for her. She'd complain about him as she took us around, making empty threats to take away his car, lamenting the fact that she could never get her son to listen or take direction. I often felt like Zahra's mom made the drives more for me than she did her own daughter; she seemed to know, somehow, that if she didn't show up for me, no one would. Of course, this was a baseless theory, one I found both comforting and embarrassing, but I'd been grateful to her nonetheless—most of all for never making me feel like a burden.

The day I realized Zahra and I were no longer friends was the day I arrived at the after-school pickup before she did. I'd seen Zahra's mom, waved hello. I'd just begun walking over to her car when Zahra showed up and said *Oh my God, stop following me around everywhere. And for once in your life, get your own ride home.* That was the day she tore off my head and filled me with a humiliation so dense I nearly sank straight into the earth. There were some things I had not yet learned how to forget.

Slowly, I turned around.

Ali was staring at me. Ali the liar, standing there lying to my face.

"Since when," I said to him, "do you pick up your sister from school?"

He frowned. "I pick her up all the time."

Liar.

He could only dare to lie like this because he had no idea that my own mom never took me anywhere anymore. Up until two months ago I'd sat beside his sister in his mother's red minivan every single day; I still saw his mom's car come and go in the school parking lot.

I narrowed my eyes at him.

It was becoming clear to me now that there was something Ali had come here to say, and I decided to give him the chance to say it before I disappeared from his life—because I intended to disappear, this time for good. I didn't want to be accosted by Zahra anymore. I was sick of her accusations, sick of being made to feel like a terrible person—in perpetuity—for something I hadn't even done.

I took an unsteady breath.

Ali had lied to me, and though I saw no point in exposing his lie, I did not also see the point in making this easy for him. Instead, I kept my eyes on his, the deep wells of brown, the shatteringly dark lashes. Mostly I stared at his face so I wouldn't stare at anything else; I worried he'd catch me grazing his neck with my eyes, touching his shoulders with the tilt of my head.

He'd always been hard to ignore.

Ali loved soccer, was religious about the sport not unlike many men—especially Iranian men—but his obsession was unique in that he actually played the sport, and kicking that ball around had honed his body into something beautiful. I knew this because I had seen him, on a single occasion, by pure accident, without his shirt on. I had walked the hallowed halls of the shrine that was his home for six years, had been attacked by the evidence of his existence since I was eleven. I didn't even need to see him without his clothes on to know why the female contingent loved him. He was a rare specimen. And it had always driven Zahra insane.

Finally, Ali broke.

"What?" he said, and sighed. "Why are you looking at me like that?"

"Why did you come here?"

He turned away, shoved both hands through his hair. Most guys wore so much gel in their hair these days you could break the strands with a hammer. Ali did not appear to care for this trend.

"I didn't know," he said finally. "About your dad."

I held my breath.

"I wanted to apologize. For all of it. For not knowing. For forgetting about Mehdi. I just—I needed to say it."

My anger died on the spot. The feeling deserted me so quickly I felt light-headed in its absence. Limp.

"Oh," I said. "That's okay. There's no reason for you to know things about my life."

Ali exhaled, frustrated. "I just wish I'd known. Sometimes I ask Zahra how you're doing, but she never tells me much."

"Hey, maybe in the future"—I hesitated—"maybe you shouldn't talk to Zahra about me. At all. She's not— She's getting the wrong idea."

Ali frowned. "I don't talk to her about you. I almost never talk to her about you. But after I left the hospital I went to pick her up from school, and she saw your backpack in my car. When she asked me about it I told her I'd given you a ride to the hospital."

"Oh."

"And, I mean, she asked me what happened, and I explained, and then I asked her about your dad and then . . ." He trailed off. His face cleared, realization imminent.

"Okay. Yeah, I might've asked her a lot of questions about you last night." He looked over his shoulder suddenly. "Speaking of which, I should probably go. She's waiting for me."

I nodded, looked at nothing. And then I swallowed my pride and said, "When you see her, will you please tell her that there's nothing happening between us?"

Ali spun back around like I'd slapped him. "What?"

"Or maybe you can tell her that nothing *ever* happened between us? Because she thinks"—I shook my head—"I don't know, she came up to me today, and she was really upset. She seemed to think that we, that, I don't know—"

"Are you joking?" Ali blinked, stunned, took a step back. "Please tell me you're joking."

"What? Why?"

"I can't believe you're still doing this. I can't believe you're still letting her do this to you, even now, when she's not even— Listen, Shadi, I don't need anyone else's permission to live my own life. And you shouldn't, either."

"She's not just anyone else," I said quietly. "She's your sister."

"I know she's my sister."

"Ali—"

"Listen, I don't care, okay? This isn't about us. You told me to jump off a cliff, and I did. I jumped off a fucking cliff. I cut myself out of your life because you asked me to, because you can't see that my sister is just jealous of you, that she's always been jealous of you, and can't stand the idea of you being happy."

Suddenly, I couldn't breathe.

"I'm not trying to change your mind anymore," he said. "All right? I moved on. And if I'm standing here right now asking questions it's only because I'm worried about you, because we used to be friends."

I flinched. "I know that."

"Then stop letting my sister dictate the terms of your life. Or mine, for that matter. Make your own choices."

"Ali, she was my friend," I said. "My best friend."

"Your *best friend*. Wow. Okay." He nodded, then laughed. "Tell me something, Shadi—what kind of best friend doesn't want you to be happy? What kind of best friend doesn't care if she hurts you? What kind of best friend denies you the right to make decisions for yourself?"

"That isn't fair," I said, "it wasn't that simple—"

"We were friends, too, weren't we? Why didn't I get a vote?"

I looked up at him then, caught the flash of pain in his eyes before it disappeared. I thought to say something, wanted to say something, and I never had the chance.

Ali laughed.

He laughed, dragged his hands down his face, stared up at the sky. He seemed to be laughing at something only he understood. I watched as his body went slack, as the light left his eyes. He took a steadying breath, stared into the distance as he exhaled. When Ali finally met my eyes again he looked tired. He smiled, and it broke my heart.

"Don't worry," he said. "I'll tell my sister that nothing ever happened between us."

I stared at him. Heat was pushing up my throat again, pressing against my eyes, and I knew I couldn't take much more of this. I nodded toward the long walk that awaited me.

"I should get going."

"Right. Yeah." He clapped his hands together. Took a step back. "Okay."

I'd just turned to leave when I heard him say—

"Wait."

It was soft, uncertain.

I turned back around, the question in my eyes.

Ali moved toward me again. His face was different now, worried. "Last night," he said, "when I asked you if you were okay—you said no."

My hesitant smile disappeared. My face became a mask. "I'm sorry I said that. I shouldn't have said that."

"Don't— Shadi, don't apologize. I just wanted to know— are you okay now?"

"Oh. Yeah." I took a deep breath, forced a smile back on my face, swallowed down the heat, willed my eyes to remain dry. "Yeah. Great."

"Is your mom okay?"

"Yeah, she's great, too." I nodded. "So much better. Thanks."

He was about to say something else, but I couldn't take it anymore. I cut him off in a rush, terrified the tremble would return to my lips.

"I have to go, actually. I need to get home for dinner. My mom's waiting for me."

"Oh," he said, surprised. "That's . . . great."

"Yeah," I said again, eyes still dry, legs still working. "Really great."

FOURTEEN

When I got home, the house was dark.

I closed the door behind me, the familiar whine of an ungreased hinge preceding the heavy close. I leaned back against the door, rested my head against the cheap wood. I smelled new paint, stale air, the faint aroma of Windex. We'd moved into this sterile rental not long after my brother died. It had become impossible to live in a place that housed the museum of his life, the modest bedroom from which my father would drag my mother's prone, sobbing body every night. I saw her with my own eyes only once, just once before my father chased me out, shouting at me to go back to bed. My mother was curled on the floor of my brother's room, banging her head against the baseboard, begging God to be merciful and kill her.

Somehow, through the power of violent self-delusion, my

parents thought we wouldn't hear them fighting late at night, thought we wouldn't have ways of seeing them in the hallway, thought we wouldn't hear my father begging my mother to come back to bed, begging in a voice I'd never known him to possess. *Come back, come back, come back, come back.*

She'd slapped him in the face.

She'd thrown feeble, desperate punches at his chest, clawing at him until he finally let go, let her sink to the floor. I watched from a half-inch opening in my bedroom door, my heart pounding so hard I could barely breathe. In the dead of night my parents became strangers, each utterly transformed into versions of themselves I did not know.

I watched my father fall to his knees before my mother, a penitent dictator. I watched my mother reduce him to ash.

On the morning my father announced we were moving, no one even lifted their heads. There were no questions, no discussions.

There was no need.

We left that place behind, did not drive past our old street, did not discuss the hours my mother now spent in her closet. But when I closed my eyes I still heard her voice; I still saw her desperate, inhuman face. *Kill me, dear God*, she'd cry. She'd slap herself in the chest, drag fingernails down her face. Mano bokosho az een donya bebar. *Kill me and take me away from this world.*

I turned on the lights.

I dropped my backpack by the door, kicked off my shoes.

My chest was tightening like a vise around my lungs, my vision blurring. In my mind I saw a stethoscope, a brown smudge, a scuffed gold wedding band.

Has she ever said anything to make you think she might be a danger to herself?

I felt heavy and cold.

I stared at an ancient, painted nail buried in the wall by the door, stood in the entryway staring at it for what felt like forever. I didn't know what to do with myself. I was hungry, I had homework, I needed to shower, I had to find my phone, I wanted to put on a sweater, and I needed to change the bandage on my knee, the wound of which had been throbbing since yesterday. I was cold and damp and shivering, my head hot, my hands unsteady. I had a thousand human needs that needed tending to and I felt paralyzed by the weight of those needs, felt impotent in the face of all that I required. I'd been starting to scare myself lately, worrying that I perhaps I wasn't eating enough or sleeping enough. I couldn't afford to fall apart, which meant I needed to do better, but my heart and mind were so full these days they were stretching at the seams, leaving little room for the efforts I'd once made to participate in my own life, in my own interests.

Somehow, I dragged myself upstairs.

I locked myself in the bathroom and tugged off my scarf, stripped off my clothes, stepped into a scalding shower. I stood under the water until my legs could no longer hold my weight, sat down on the shower floor until my head grew heavy.

I pressed my forehead to the tile, the rough grout abrading my skin. I breathed deep, inhaling water. Closed my eyes.

Dear God, I thought. *Help me.*

My tears made no sound.

I didn't know how long I spent there, my body poorly heated by a weak showerhead, didn't know how long I'd been crying. I'd gone back in time, turned into a fetus, laid there on the shower floor like an infant unclaimed. Soundless sobs wracked my body, tore open my chest. I did not know what to do with all this pain. I did not know whether I wanted to be born.

I was startled suddenly by a sharp knock at the door.

Another knock—no, a heavy pounding—and I was upright so fast I nearly slipped in the tub. My mind had grown accustomed to panic and went there easily now, with little encouragement. My heart was racing, my eyes felt swollen. I scrubbed violently at my face, made a concerted effort to remain calm. When I felt ready, I turned off the water.

"Yes?"

"You've been in there for like two hours," my sister said. "I need to use the bathroom." I marveled at the exaggeration. Then, distracted, I wondered when she'd arrived home, what time it was, whether my mother was back from work.

"You can use the other bathroom," I said, clinging to the plastic shower curtain. "I'm almost done."

"Let me in," she said. "I don't want to keep shouting."

That was unusual for Shayda.

Gingerly, I stepped out of the shower, grabbed a fresh towel, and unlocked the bathroom door. I'd just jumped back into the tub and pulled the shower curtain closed when I heard the door rattle and swing open.

"Okay get out, right now," my sister said sharply.

"I'm about to," I said, hastily wrapping the towel around my body. "Why? What's going on?"

"Hassan's mom is here."

"So?" I said. And then: "*Oh.*"

"Yes. Exactly. So get your lazy ass out of the shower and come make tea."

I frowned, about to argue, then changed my mind. I realized that, in her own weird way, Shayda was asking for my help. She wanted me around for support during a stressful situation.

I was touched.

I felt it in truth, like a finger of heat pressed to my chest. But when she left half a second later, slamming the door so hard I felt the shower rod shake, I was decidedly less enthused. Still, it was something.

Shayda really seemed to despise me most days.

It was easy to dismiss our strained relationship with a shrug and a platitude about how she and I were just different, but I knew it was more complicated than that. We'd never been very close, but our paths had only recently split in earnest, and only because we couldn't agree on a single matter of great importance.

I blamed my father, unequivocally, for Mehdi's death.

Shayda did not.

I'd been stunned by her position on the matter. I'd never before had cause to know, in detail, our many differences, hadn't reason to ask Shayda what she considered most important in life, faith, family. I'd never known exactly how she felt about dogma, or our parents, or even how harshly she'd judged our brother's life. But when Mehdi died, the four of us left behind were forced to tear ourselves open, to examine the innards that made us tick. Death demanded we question the privately held, still-forming philosophies that shaped our hearts. We studied one another's weak flesh and festering minds in the harsh, unflattering light of a midday sun, and when the moon rose, we'd found ourselves alone on different quadrants of the earth. I stood as far away from my sister as my mother did from my father, and I'd spent the last year trying and failing to bridge those distances.

The trouble was, I was often the only one making the effort.

I tiptoed to my bedroom in a towel, combed my fingers through damp, clean hair. The bandage on my chin had come off in the shower, and I was happy to discover the wound beginning to heal. Gingerly, I touched the cut with the tips of my fingers, tapping at the pain as I slid open my closet door, studied the contents within.

Unlike me, Shayda was eager to get married.

She'd fought with my mom over this, insisting it was

something she wanted. She'd already picked out the guy, had accepted his hand, had a five-year plan. Shayda was nineteen, in her second year at the junior college, but she was going to transfer to a local university soon, and she wanted to be engaged for the next couple of years. Her plan was to get married just after graduation. She did not want to have children, not ever. She just wanted the husband.

This plan struck most non-Muslim people as either stupid or bizarre, but within many religious communities, it wasn't uncommon. A lot of people got married relatively young, or at least got engaged young. They'd get engaged for a couple of years, spend time together with the express purpose of marriage, then get married. There were happy and unhappy couples. Divorce was not taboo; we had plenty of that, too. Which—not for the first time—made me wonder about my own parents.

A single knock on my bedroom door was my only warning before Shayda barged into my room, looking overheated.

"Why aren't you dressed?" And then, taking a long look at me: "Why are your eyes all red and puffy?"

I startled, glanced in the mirror. "Oh," I said. "Allergies?"

"You don't have allergies."

"Maybe I do." I tried to laugh. "Is it really bad?"

"Whatever, I don't care," she said, distracted. "Just get dressed, please. I can't go down there without you."

"What? Why not?"

"*Because*," she said. She narrowed her eyes, pinwheeled her arms like I should understand.

I did not.

And then she shook her head, shook her head like she was talking to an idiot. "I don't want to look too eager, okay? I'm trying to be—" She waved her hand around, searching for the right word.

"Nonchalant?"

"What? Why can't you talk like a normal person?"

"I do talk like a nor—"

"God, I don't care, okay?" She cut me off. "I don't care. How do I look?"

I took a deep breath and thought of my mother, my mother, my mother. And then, carefully, I processed the scene in front of me.

Shayda was wearing a dress—long and frilly and glittery—with a shiny hijab to match. She looked nice, but extremely overdressed, a truth I wasn't sure I should impart. I didn't know how to tell her that it didn't matter how many people accompanied her as she descended the stairs; her outfit screamed the truth.

She looked too eager.

"You look really nice," I said instead.

She rolled her eyes and shot me a look so scathing it scared me a little. "Forget it, I'll go without you."

She was already at the door, turning the handle, when I said:

"What is your problem?" I could no longer keep the anger out of my voice. "I just told you that you look really nice. Why is that a bad thing?"

"I said *forget it*, Shadi. I don't want to talk about this anymore. I was stupid to even ask you to care."

"What's that supposed to mean?"

"What do you think it means?" She spun back without warning. "It means you don't care. It means you don't give a shit about anyone but yourself."

I stepped back like I'd been struck.

"That's not true," I said, but I was stunned, which made me sound uncertain, which only proved her point.

She laughed, but the sound was hollow, angry. "You don't care about anything. Not about us, not about Baba. You never talk to Maman, you never ask me anything about my life."

"I didn't know you wanted me to ask—I didn't even know you wanted to talk to me—"

Her eyes went wide. "Shadi, you're my *sister*. Who else am I supposed to talk to?"

I took a step forward and she drew suddenly back, her face flushing.

"Don't you dare try to hug me. Don't you dare try to patronize me."

"I'm not trying to patronize you, I just—"

"You have no idea how hard it's been for me this last year," she said, her eyes shining with sudden emotion. "You have no idea, Shadi." She shook her head, looked around. "Who do you think keeps the house running these days? Who do you think makes sure we have food in the fridge? Who do you think takes out the trash, cleans the kitchen, brings in the mail, sorts the bills, makes sure Maman has gas in her car, cashes her checks, makes sure Baba's insurance is going through?"

"Shayda—"

"*Me*, Shadi." She stabbed a finger at her chest. "It's me. And you don't lift a finger to help. You don't even pretend to give a shit. You have no idea what I've been going through or how much I have to do every day or even this"—she waved her hands around—"this, today, with Hassan." She laughed, suddenly, sounded hysterical. "You don't even know what's happening, do you? You've never asked me a single question about him. You know literally nothing about my life, and you couldn't care less."

"Of course I care. Shayda, I want to know—please, listen to me—"

"No—I'm *sick* of how selfish you've been. I'm sick and tired of it. You're out doing God-knows-what with Ali, of all people, who treats the rest of us like shit, who hasn't even talked to us in like a year—and you never, *ever* want to know how Baba is doing. You never visit him at the hospital. You don't even care about him. You *want* him to die. Don't you? *Don't you?*"

She was just screaming at me now, her painted lips curving around the awful sounds. I'd frozen in place, my compassion turning to dust as I imagined my mother sitting downstairs, pretending not to hear some distorted version of this in front of her guest. I was picturing her mortification, her horror.

"Please," I said quietly. "Please stop shouting."

She would not.

"You *want* our family to fall apart. You want our parents to get a divorce. After everything we've been through—after everything, you just want it all to get worse. Why? What the hell is wrong with you?"

"Shayda," I said desperately. "There are people downstairs. They can hear you. Maman will hear you."

"So you're not even going to answer my questions?" She shook her head, disgusted, and with that movement the fight left her body. She looked bereft in the aftermath. Bereft and cruel. "You're not going to answer my questions, but you're going to stand there and pretend to be righteous, pretend to be better than me, than all the rest of us?"

"Shayda. Stop."

"You didn't even cry at his funeral," she said, and I heard her breath hitch. "Sometimes I think you don't even care that he's dead."

I was suddenly breathing so hard I thought my chest would explode. I stared at the carpet under my feet, tried desperately to keep my anger in check. This time, I failed.

"*Get out.*"

"What?" She startled.

"Get out. Get out of my room. Go get married. Good luck."

"I'm not getting married," she said, still confused. "I'm just—"

I looked up, locked eyes with her. She visibly flinched.

"You don't know anything about me, Shayda. You don't know anything at all." I walked past her, yanked open the door. "Now leave."

She wouldn't.

So I did.

I pulled on a pair of jeans and an old hoodie, tugged a wool beanie over my wet hair. Shayda was telling me that I'd lost my mind, that I'd officially gone insane, that I couldn't go downstairs looking like that without embarrassing her, and that I couldn't leave without saying hello to Hassan's mom or else disrespect their entire family, and that this—*this*—was only further proof that I didn't care about anyone but myself, that I was a monster, a monster of a human being who didn't care about anyone, didn't care about *anyone*—

These were the words she shouted at me as I barreled down the stairs.

My mother stood erect, waiting for me as I entered the living room, the look on her face violent enough to commit a double homicide.

I'd missed that look.

"I'm sorry," I said breathlessly, and forced a smile.

I did my best to make quick work of the extremely polite and overly formal hellos and apologies necessary, my stilted, accented Farsi making the scene even more ridiculous. I thanked the woman I assumed was Hassan's mom for honoring our home with her presence, for being gracious enough to overlook my appearance, and to please, please sit down and make herself comfortable. Her lips kept twitching as I talked, as she took me in, staring at me as though she were trying hard not to laugh.

My mother sighed.

But when I started putting on my shoes, she sharpened.

"Koja dari miri?" she said. *Where are you going?*

I knew it was only out of courtesy for her guest that she didn't rip open my spleen right there on the living room floor, and it filled me with no small amount of joy to see her like this, something like herself. I didn't mind at all that she would no doubt kill me later.

"I forgot my phone at Zahra's house," I said quickly, affecting nonchalance. Insouciance. Indifference. I hated Shayda. "I need to run back and grab it."

"Alaan?" *Right now?*

My mother peered out the window, at the increasing darkness. Zahra's house wasn't far from here, only about four streets down. For a few months Zahra's proximity to our new house had been the only fringe benefit in moving. Three months ago, when I'd been sent to the nurse's office after passing out in the middle of second period, I couldn't get ahold of anyone. Instead, I called Zahra's mom, who sent her husband to pick me up. He left work, bought me five different kinds of medicine I didn't need, and let me sleep in Zahra's bed. I was so astonished by their kindness I wrote them a letter right there in Zahra's bedroom, at her desk, using her paper and pen. It was a long letter, the contents of which were an exaggeration of emotion, embarrassing in their sincerity. I'd left the letter in their mailbox. Walked home. Said nothing to my own family about my day.

Zahra told me, when I went back to school, that her parents had found my letter. She told me at lunch. She kept peering at me over her sandwich, looking at me like she'd never seen me properly before, like maybe I was crazy.

"That was a weird letter," she'd said, and laughed. She kept laughing. *My parents thought it was sweet, but I thought it was so funny. It was a joke, right?*

My mom didn't know that Zahra and I were no longer friends.

I never told her what happened, because telling my mom what happened would only cause her to worry about me, which would break my vow to spare her the need to ever worry about me. I didn't want her to worry. Not about me. Not about anyone. And yet—

Even in this, I was occasionally a failure.

My mother was still staring out the window, and I could tell she was about to forbid me from leaving the house. I could feel it, could see the words forming—

"Zahra's waiting for me," I said quickly. "I'll just run there and be back. Ten minutes!"

I slammed the door shut behind me.

FIFTEEN

The day my brother died, my mother was making ghormeh sabzi. The kitchen was warm with the heat of the stove, the air heavy with the smells of caramelized meat and fresh rice. I was sitting at the kitchen table, offering no assistance at all as she cleaned up the mess. I was in a daze, watching her with unusual fascination as she took apart the food processor she'd used to mince a half ton of parsley. I'd seen her do this a thousand times before—had done it myself—but that day I felt numb as I sat there. Incomprehensibly paralyzed.

My father was pacing, lecturing the air as my mother worked, as I sat. I'd tuned it out, most of it. I thought about Shayda, who was at the mosque; they had a youth group on Friday nights. I hadn't gone, despite her insistence that I accompany her, and I was regretting that decision then. I watched my mother place dirty bowls in the dishwasher, watched her shoot my father an irritated look as he stalked across the living room—a look he didn't catch. I glanced at him, at his two tufts of dark hair, at his salt-and-pepper beard.

He was in a frenzy.

That morning, my father had needed to move my brother's car, because Mehdi had blocked the garage with his Civic. My dad was in a hurry, running late for work, and asked me to fetch my brother's keys. I did, because I knew precisely where they were: in a pocket of his discarded jeans, lying on his bedroom floor. It was still early, and Mehdi, who was in college, did not have class for at least another two hours. I snuck into his room while he was sleeping, stole his car keys, crept back downstairs. Placed the keys in my father's hand.

Too often, my mind stopped there.

I could seldom convince my brain to remember what happened next. I didn't want to remember. I didn't want any of these memories, these distorted loops of sounds and images. I didn't want to remember that it was me, me who betrayed my brother. I handed those keys to my father, my father who kissed me on the cheek and said, Merci, azizam, and promptly discovered a six-pack of beer in my brother's back seat.

My dad waited all day to lose his mind.

His anger festered while he was at work, his imagination spiraling. He managed to convince himself of all kinds of things, all without my brother's assistance, without the clarity that might be provided by a single conversation. I'd heard his theories that night, sitting at the kitchen table while my mother stirred the stew with a wooden spoon.

"He's drinking, doing drugs, maybe selling drugs—"

"*Mansour.*" My mother spun around, horrified. "Een harfa chiyeh? We don't know what happened," she'd said in Farsi. "There's still a chance the alcohol didn't even belong to Mehdi."

My father laughed out loud at that. His eyes were flinty, furious.

My mother was angry, too, but she said she wanted to wait until Mehdi got home, wanted to give him a chance to explain himself.

Calm down, she said.

My dad very nearly exploded at the suggestion.

Let's talk to him first, she said.

My father went purple.

Talk to him? Talk to him? I don't need to talk to him. You think I don't know? You think I don't know? He thinks I'm an idiot, that he can hide things from me, that I don't know what he smells like every day, what his eyes look like? Everyone thinks I'm stupid, that I don't know what's going on? Talk to him? Talk to him about what?

My brother hadn't been home all day.

My parents were still waiting for him to get back, waiting to ambush him. I'd let him know, of course. I'd texted him. Told him what happened.

I'm so sorry, I'd written.

I'm so sorry

I didn't know

Baba had to go to work
I didn't know
I'm so sorry
I'm so, so so so sorry
Mehdi, I'm so sorry

It's okay, he'd written back.
It's not your fault.

I'd stared at that message a thousand times, pressed the screen to my throat on desperate nights. I could never have known how things would escalate. Could never have anticipated the proceeding argument, the explosive screaming match that met my brother's reluctant arrival back home.

It was late.

I remember, when my dad threw open the front door, that the crickets would not quiet. Streetlamps were bright and blurry, streaking the sky in the distance, cold air piercing everything. I remember, when my father told him to get out, Mehdi did not hesitate. My mother screamed. My brother shoved on his shoes, his face grim with determination, and though my mother begged him to be reasonable, begged him to come back inside, Mehdi did not hear her. He wasn't looking at my mother. He was looking at my father, my prideful father who did not seem to understand that he and his son suffered from the same affliction, that my brother would not break.

Mehdi left.

My mother chased her firstborn child into the dark, chased him barefoot down the driveway. My mother, for whom propriety and privacy meant a great deal, ran through our neighborhood screaming his name. If Mehdi was the sea, my father was an immovable object, human stone standing in the living room, unwilling to be eroded.

I retreated to the stairs, sat on the narrow, carpeted step with my arms wrapped around my shins, cried with my head buried in my lap.

Mehdi was killed, not ten minutes later, by a drunk driver.

I came back to my body with a sudden gasp of awareness, startling at the cold drip. Tentative raindrops tested out the sky, the trees, the slope of my nose, made way for the others. It wasn't much, just a drizzle. Still I shivered, violently.

I didn't know where I'd left my phone.

I had no intention of actually looking for it; I just wanted an excuse to walk, clear my head, think in peace—and I hoped that the *mehmooni* taking place at my house would be diverting enough to buy me some time. My feet walked a familiar pattern, a pattern my feet knew but my mind could not remember. I stared occasionally at the sky, searching for the moon.

It was true, I thought. I did want my father to die.

My heart sagged a little more in my chest.

I realized, when I was suddenly blinded by a dot diagram of lights, that I'd walked into a local park. I'd been to this park a hundred times with Zahra, the two of us pretending to be children, sitting on swings and climbing backward up the slide. We sat in the sand and discussed school and boys and minor social dramas that held critical importance in our lives. We'd spent days here. Weekends. Untold hours of my life, gone up in flames.

My friendship with Zahra had long been imperfect.

She'd been cruel to me in a thousand small ways for years, had proven herself a fickle, disloyal friend many times over. I should've been the one to walk away, should've done it long ago. But she'd been one of the few solid things in my life, and I hadn't been ready to let go. I clung with the tips of my fingers to the fast-crumbling cliff of our friendship, and when she finally kicked me down, into the chasm, I experienced a strange, disorienting relief.

Part of me missed her fiercely.

A greater part of me did not.

I shuddered as a gust of wind tore through the park, whipping at my body. I was naked underneath this hoodie and I suddenly regretted my haphazard choices. I wrapped my arms around myself. Held on tight.

This graveyard of memories was nearly empty now, save a distant soccer field still dotted with players. The streetlights were unnecessarily aggressive, and I sat away from one, atop a bench, my legs curled under me. The bench wasn't wet, exactly, but damp with drizzle and fog, and the cold seeped through my clothes, chilling me further. A child's swing swayed gently in the breeze; I stared at it. I clasped and unclasped the old, loose cigarette rolling around in my pocket.

I'd been trying not to think about this cigarette.

I'd known it was here, tucked away in a zippered pocket; I'd known, because I left cigarettes everywhere. It was a stupid, reckless indulgence, but I couldn't seem to help it; I liked finding them in my clothes. I carried them around like some kind of talisman, smoking them only occasionally, and at first only because I was curious. I'd since developed a dangerous taste for the poison, which worried me. But I couldn't part with them.

Mehdi had stashed two large cartons of cigarettes in his closet, a bulk quantity I can only assume he purchased through a third party. I'd tossed his dirty magazines, disposed of the weed, destroyed the glass pipe, chucked the condoms into a massive garbage bin behind a grocery store.

The cigarettes, I kept.

I sighed, tucked one between my lips and left it there. I found a lighter in the pocket of my jeans, weighed it in my hand.

I knew I couldn't smoke this cigarette, no matter how much I wanted to. I had to get home soon, before my mom came looking for me and unraveled a long string of lies I did not want to acknowledge. But I wasn't ready to leave. I spun the spark wheel a few times, stared at the flame.

I thought often of the stupidity of man. One, in particular.

I thought often of my father's self-righteousness, his self-assured certainty, his unequivocal conviction that his thoughts and actions were sanctioned by God. It was perhaps true that my father had never had a drop of alcohol. I knew he regularly gave charity, never missed one of his daily prayers, fasted during Ramadan. My brother, on the other hand, had done none of those things. And yet I felt quite certain that, in the eyes of God, my brother was the better person.

I didn't mind dogma. I liked guideposts, appreciated a little structure. But I could not understand those people who disregarded the essence of faith—love, compassion, forgiveness, the necessary expansion of the soul—in favor of a set of rules, a set of rules they declared to be true divinity.

This—*this*—

I did not think Shayda and I would ever agree on this. Here was where we diverged, where our lives tore on a perforated line. She felt that my father had been right to be angry with Mehdi, that Mehdi had broken the rules, had made poor choices, had angered my father when he should've been repentant, and deliberately disrespected my mother, who begged him to stay.

He made his own choice, she'd said.

I thought it was the job of the parent to be smarter than the child, I'd said. I thought it was the job of the parent to protect their child from harm, I'd said. I thought it was the job of the parent to lead by example, I'd said.

She'd screamed at me. Thrown me out of her room. We'd never talked about Mehdi again, not until tonight.

I sighed, ran my thumb over the top of the lighter. Spun the starter.

Spark and flame.

Spark and flame.

And what about me? I thought. What did it make me, if I sat around, cold and without compassion, hoping for my father to die? Did that make me any different from him?

Or just worse?

I sat up suddenly, startled free of my reverie by a sharp motion, a blur of movement. A body sat down heavily on the seat beside me, and I turned to stare at it. Him.

Ali was holding my cigarette, which he'd snatched from my lips.

"Give that back," I said quietly.

He laughed.

I'd wondered, when I saw the brilliantly lit soccer field, whether Ali might not be out there tonight. He lived close by. He played soccer. I didn't know exactly what he played—it was some kind of local, intramural team—but my thoughts ended there, did not build a bridge elsewhere. The field was situated far from my bench, and I'd not determined there to be a high probability of our worlds colliding.

So I was surprised.

He took the lighter from my limp hand, his fingers grazing my palm in the process. I held my breath as he lit the cigarette I would not smoke, put it between his lips. It was all I could think as I watched him smoke it, that the cigarette touching his mouth had been touching mine not a moment ago.

"This is so bad for you," he said, exhaling with an elegance attained only with practice. "You shouldn't smoke these things."

He offered me the cigarette without turning his head, and when I whispered, "No, thank you," he smiled.

He still wasn't looking at me; he was staring into the darkness. I found his silence fascinating. His appearance, here, confusing.

"What are you doing here?" I asked.

"What are *you* doing here?" he said, and laughed. "I live here." He gestured, generally, at nothing. "You know. Around here."

"Right." I took a deep breath. "Yeah."

He took another drag on the cigarette. "So," he said, exhaling a neat line of smoke. "You want to tell me why you're stalking me?"

"What?" I said sharply. I felt my face heat. "I'm not stalking you."

"No?" He turned a little in his seat, looked me up and down. He was almost smiling. "Then why do you look like you're undercover?"

I shook my head. Looked away. "It's a long story."

"I've got time."

"It's a stupid story," I amended.

"Even better."

"My sister is getting married."

Ali choked, started coughing violently. He tossed the cigarette to the ground, stamped it out with his foot. Kept coughing. Ali was about to die of asphyxiation, and I was suddenly very close to laughing. I also noticed, for the first time, what he was wearing: cleats and shorts, a blue soccer jersey. It was freezing out, and his arms and legs were bare and he didn't seem at all bothered by the temperature. The streetlamps bolstered the wan moonlight, sculpting his body in the darkness. I watched him press the heels of his hands to his tearing eyes, watched as the muscles in his arms tightened, released under his skin. When he finally sat back and took a normal, steadying breath, my head felt uncomfortably hot.

"Oh my God," he said. Another cough. "Is your sister *insane*?"

I was fully smiling now, rare for me. "She's not getting married this second. But she's on her way, I guess. Picked out the guy."

"*Picked out the guy*? What does that even mean? And what does any of that have to do with you looking like a"—he gestured at me, my face—"getaway driver?"

I laughed. I missed this version of us, the easy conversations we'd once had. Ali and I had always been so comfortable together, and remembering that now—remembering what I'd lost—made my smile feel suddenly brittle. I shook my head to clear it.

"He came khastegari," I said. "She accepted. And tonight h—"

"Wait, what's *khastegari*?"

I frowned, turned to face him. "Since when do you not know how to speak Farsi?"

Ali shrugged. "I always spoke Farsi like a child."

"Oh." I was still frowning. "Well, it just means he proposed."

"But you said she picked him out. Like a peach at the grocery store."

"Well, yeah, I mean, lots of guys propose," I said, squinting up at the blinking light of an airplane. "But she picked him."

"Shadi, I have no idea what you're talking about. I don't know any guys who propose."

I laughed again.

He didn't.

"I'm serious," he said. "This sounds fake. It sounds like you're describing *The Bachelor* in reverse."

"*The Bachelorette*."

"Whatever."

"Yeah, I guess it's sort of like that. Sort of." I frowned again. Turned to face him, again. "You've really never heard of khastegari?"

"Why on earth would I know what that means?"

"I don't know." I shrugged. "It's a pretty common thing."

"You mean this is normal? This happens all the time? More than one guy will ask the same girl to marry him and then just stand around waiting until she chooses?"

I laughed. "No."

"Thank God."

"But, I mean, sometimes." I took a sharp breath. I was beginning to feel self-conscious. "Sometimes that happens."

"That sounds insane."

"It's not completely insane," I said, no longer smiling.

Ali turned in his seat without warning, one of his arms bracing the back of the bench. He was studying my face from an uncomfortably close distance when he said:

"Holy shit. Are these assholes kasigaring you, too?"

"It's khastegari."

"Whatever."

"They're not assholes."

"*Oh my God.*" He sat back against the bench, stared at me, slack-jawed. "Who would propose to you? You're seventeen. How is that not illegal?"

I bristled.

Who would propose to you? was possibly the most offensive question I'd ever been asked, and I'd been asked a great deal of offensive questions.

"First of all, I'll be eighteen in like a month."

"Still illegal!"

"Listen," I said, irritated. "You've clearly been away from the mosque for too long, because you don't seem to understand how this works. You don't just *get married*. Proposing is a formality, a custom. A khastegari is basically just a request to date, to get to know each other with the specific intention of possibly, one day—maybe even years into the future—getting married. It's considered a courtesy. Dating done properly, respectfully, with honorable intentions."

He wasn't listening to me. "How many guys kassgaried you?"

"*Khastegari*."

"How many?"

I hesitated.

"Two?" His eyes widened. "Three?"

I looked away.

"*More than three?*"

"Five."

"Holy fucking hell." He stiffened and stared at me, stared at me out of the corner of his eye like he'd never seen me before. Like I'd contracted leprosy.

None of this was flattering.

"You're telling me that there are five dudes just waiting around to see if you'll choose one of them?"

I sighed.

"There are five dudes just sitting at home, staring at the wall, waiting for you to decide which one of them gets to marry you?"

I rolled my eyes.

"Wait." He laughed. "Do these guys even know you smoke? Do they know you wander around abandoned playgrounds at night, stalking innocent men?"

I shot him a hard look. "Okay, I think I should go."

I stood up and he stopped me, his hand curving around my forearm. I stared, surprised by the scene sketched poorly in the uneven light, surprised by the weight of such a simple touch.

"Wait," he said. He was no longer smiling. "Wait a second."

I sat back down, tugged at my beanie.

"What?" I said, still irritated.

"You're not actually going to marry one of these guys, right?"

I looked up at that, at the horror on his face. I was angry with him, suddenly. Angry with him for making me feel small, for shattering what little was left of my vanity. "I thought you said I shouldn't need anyone else's permission to live my own life."

He flinched at that. Hesitated.

"This is different," he said. "This just seems wrong."

"Why is it wrong? What if I actually like one of them? What if it's actually something I want?"

His eyebrows flew up. He seemed suddenly unmoored. "Do you?"

"Do I what?"

"Do you—I mean—do you actually like one of them?"

I almost laughed.

"Why would I tell you, even if I did? You've just spent this entire conversation horrified by the idea that anyone would even consider marrying me, and now you want me to dissect the inner workings of my heart for you?"

His eyes widened. "Shadi, I just—I care about you. You're like— I mean, I'd be upset if this were happening to my sister, too, you know?" He straightened. "Wait, there aren't dudes kargarying my sister, are there?"

I went still. "No."

"No one at all?"

"I don't know," I said. "I haven't talked to Zahra in a long time."

"But, like, to the best of your knowledge?"

"No."

"Huh." He looked out into the night. "I think I'm offended."

"Yeah." I tried to laugh.

I sighed, instead.

The first time someone's mother proposed to my mother the whole thing struck me as unbelievably funny, and I shared the story with Zahra, shared it so we could analyze this strange situation and laugh about it together. The second khastegari, too. But after the third one, Zahra threw up a wall. She started making fun of me, started wondering aloud why any of these guys would ever be interested in me. And I, because I did not want to fight with Zahra, would laugh along with her, insist she was right. I'd always agree that it didn't make sense that anyone would be interested in me.

"Well, it's because you have green eyes," she'd said to me once. *Everyone is obsessed with your eyes. It's so dumb.*

It was true.

People were obsessed with my eyes, and it was dumb. Still, I should've known then. I should've seen it then, that our friendship was fast approaching its expiration date. My problem was that I didn't know friendships could have an expiration date at all.

"Hey," Ali said quietly, the sound of his voice startling me back to the present. "I didn't mean to insult you. Honestly. That wasn't my intention."

"Yeah," I said, whispered the word into the darkness.

I couldn't look at him anymore. I was tired. I was growing weary of jokes made at my expense, growing weary of carrying untold weight. I felt so heavy some days that I could hardly get out of bed, and I found it increasingly difficult to take so many different hits on a daily basis. My body had worn thin, lacked refuge. I no longer knew where I might fall apart in peace.

"Sometimes," I said softly, "I wish I could just leave."

"Leave where? Your parents' house?"

"Just leave," I said, staring up at the night sky. "Start walking and never, ever stop."

Ali was quiet for a long time. I'd begun to deeply regret my entire conversation with him when he said, softly:

"Why?"

I turned to face him and realized he was sitting close to me, much closer than before. I nearly jumped out of my skin. We locked eyes and he made as if to speak, his lips parting for the briefest moment before they froze like that, a breath apart. He was just staring at me now, looking into my eyes with a startling intensity. I felt fear skitter through my blood.

His voice was different—almost unrecognizable—when he said, "Were you crying?"

Too fast, I turned away.

"Is that what you were doing out here?" A little louder now, a little sharper. "Shadi?"

I felt it then, felt the awful, burning threat, felt it building inside me again. I swallowed it down, tried to regain my composure.

Ali touched my arm, gently, and I stilled at the sensation. Could not meet his eyes.

"Hey," he said. "What's going on? What happened?"

The heat would not abate. It was ravenous again, hungry and terrible, pooling in my gut, my throat, behind my eyes. I'd tried for months to keep everything inside, to say nothing, speak to no one, soldier through. For nearly a year I'd held my breath, stitched closed my lips, devoured myself until I could not manage another bite. I'd not known the limits of my own body at the onset, had not known how long it would take to digest pain, had not realized I might not be able to contain it or that it might continue to multiply. I spent every day standing at the edge of a terrifying precipice, peering into the abyss, wanting, not wanting to plummet.

When his fingers grazed my cheek, I stopped breathing.

"Shadi," he whispered. "Look at me."

He took my face in his hands, pinned me in place with his eyes and I, I was so desperate to exhale this pain that I could not bring myself to break away. I was shaking, my heart trembling in my chest. Even now I was trying to push it all back, pretend it away, pull myself together, but there was something about his skin against my skin, the heat radiating from his body—that broke the last of my self-control.

When I started sobbing, he froze.

And then, before I could take another breath, he pulled me into his arms.

I was crying so hard I couldn't speak, could hardly drag air into my lungs. I collapsed against him, bones shuddering, and was surprised to feel his skin against my face. His jersey was a V-neck, exposing a triangle of his chest to the night, to my cheek. I pressed my face against that heat, wet eyelashes fluttering against his throat, listened to his heart pound recklessly. My hands were caught between us, the thin jersey doing little to conceal his body from mine. He was warm and solid and strong and he was holding me in his arms like he needed me there, like he'd hold me forever if I wanted.

It all felt like a strange dream.

I might've never let go if it hadn't been for my brain, for my stuttering brain, for my slowly dawning embarrassment. Only after, after my tears slowed, after untold minutes had elapsed, after I'd spent the heat in my heart on a single purchase did I realize I'd just fallen apart on a guy I had no right to touch, no right to burden with my tears or my pain.

I tore away suddenly, gasping a hundred apologies.

I wiped at my eyes, scrubbed at my face. I was suddenly mortified, afraid to look at him. Silence descended, expanded in the darkness, grew thick with tension. And when I finally dared to look up, I was surprised.

Ali looked shaken.

He was breathing so hard I could see it, could see his chest move up and down, up and down. He stared at me like he'd seen a ghost, witnessed a murder. He was still staring at me when he touched my elbow, traced a line down my arm, took my hand, tugged me forward.

Kissed me.

Heat, soft, silk. His hand was under my chin, tilting me up, breaking me open. I didn't understand, didn't know what to do with my hands. I had never been touched like this, had never felt anything like this, was defenseless in the face of it. He dragged his fingers down the side of my neck, my shoulder, grabbed at my waist, my sweater pulling, bunching in his fist. My heart was pounding dangerously in my chest, harder and faster than I'd ever felt it and I gasped as he moved against me, gasped as I drowned, went boneless as he broke away, kissed my throat, tasted the salt of my skin. A whisper, a whisper of my name and a hand behind my head and then a sudden, desperate explosion in my chest. He kissed me with a fire I'd never, never, I'd never, I'd gone limp, trembling everywhere, my brain failing to spark a thought.

I pulled back, backed away, fell off the earth.

I braced my liquid body against the bench, unable to breathe, certain I would never again be able to stand. I did not understand what had just happened, did not know how it happened. I only knew that it was probably bad. Probably very bad. Almost certainly, maybe, probably a mistake.

Ali looked at me, looked at me and then looked away,

stood up too quickly, pushed both hands through his hair. He looked panicked.

"Oh my God," he said, shaking his head. "Oh my God. I'm sorry. I'm so sorry. I don't—"

He couldn't catch his breath, I could see it from here, even in this half-light. He looked as shaken as I felt, and his disorder comforted me, made me feel less adrift. Less insane.

I stumbled to my feet, unsteady.

I had to leave. I knew that much, knew I had to go home, get there somehow, but my heart would not calm down. My head was spinning. No one had ever kissed me before. No one had ever touched me before, not like that, not like this, not like *this*, here, he was here again, his hands around my face again, his mouth soft and hot and tasting faintly of cigarettes. My knees nearly gave out as he held me, parted my lips with his, kissed me so deeply I cried out, made a sound I didn't even know existed. I couldn't believe this was happening. I felt certain I was dreaming, my mind failing me. He kissed my cheek, my chin, his teeth grazed my jaw, his arms drawing me tighter, closer. I felt every inch of him under my hands, felt him move, felt his body harden into a solid weight, a wall of lean muscle. The scent of him, his skin, hit me, confused me. I breathed him in like something essential, the resulting sensation so heady it shattered something vital inside of me, startled my consciousness back to life.

This was too much.

I had no idea what I was doing. I had no idea what I'd

just undone. I needed space, needed time, needed to breathe.

I broke away desperately, gasping for air.

My hands were shaking. Ali was breathing hard. He looked unsteady as he stood there, closed his eyes. Opened them.

"Shadi," he said. "Shadi."

I shook my head. Shook my head over and over and over again.

"I'm sorry," he was saying. "I'm—I didn't mean—"

I ran home.

SIXTEEN

I was a corpse lying in bed, face pointed up at the ceiling, my body frozen and unwilling to warm. I watched, as if from outside of myself, as the moon stole through the slats of my poorly designed blinds, scattering light across my popcorn ceiling, creating uncanny constellations.

My father was coming home tomorrow.

I discovered this upon arrival, my brain mostly soup. I got caught in a sudden, torrential rain as I ran home, the resulting effects of which were nothing short of a miracle. I was soaked through, sopping wet and pathetic, and my mother was too busy berating me for my thoughtlessness to notice the evidence of my recent tears or worse, infinitely worse: the proof of someone else's mouth on my lips, my cheeks, my chin, my throat. Hands, hands all over my body.

I was burning up under the wet, feeling feverish. I was

done, what I'd shower, hurried into warm clothes, forced to sit
needed, ~ n with a hot cup of tea. I sank into the unexpected
     rt, savored the attentions I'd long been terrified to
    act from my mother. She and my sister didn't even seem
to remember the awful scene from earlier, the two of them too
distracted by good news, good news I nearly choked on, hot tea
scalding my throat.

My father was coming home tomorrow.

I couldn't stop staring at my mother, at the smile on her
face. I'd thought she and I had a tacit understanding of the
situation. I'd thought we were on the same page. But she
seemed happy about the news, seemed grateful.

I'd frozen as she shared it, chiseled a smile onto my face.

Et tu, Brute? I thought.

I'd been so certain he would die. His most recent stint
in the hospital had lasted two weeks; everyone expected the
worst. I'd made plans for his death, had imagined my future
in the wake of his absence. It had seemed to me like a foregone
conclusion that my father would die. His first heart attack had
seemed to me a kind of poetic justice, the kind meted out by
the Most Just, made possible by Providence.

Dear God, I thought. *Am I being punished for kissing a boy?*

I'd been listening, of course, had always been listening to
the details my mother and sister provided about my father's
situation. After his first heart attack they'd done something
called a coronary angiography, which helped them determine
where, exactly, the blockage had occurred. After that they

placed a stent in his heart, a relatively straightforward procedure that involved inserting a piece of metal inside a blocked artery to help open the valve and increase blood flow to the heart. It seemed, at the time, like a scary procedure, but he was discharged a few days later, and after a couple of nights at home, was cleared to go back to work. Everyone thought he'd be all right.

When the second heart attack hit, things got complicated.

This one was worse. More aggressive.

A blood clot developed where the stent had been placed, shutting everything down. There was real fear now, even in the doctors' voices, about how such an occurrence was extremely rare, how my father might be at greater risk than they suspected. Suddenly there was talk of open-heart surgery. Suddenly he was being examined for more than a heart attack—he was being examined for heart disease.

It was confusing.

My father was a healthy man who didn't smoke or drink or eat a great deal of red meat. He exercised regularly and looked pretty fit for his age. But his cholesterol levels had suddenly skyrocketed, something his doctor determined was a result of crushing external stress. Emotional stress.

The doctors really wanted to avoid open-heart surgery. It was an extreme surgery, with crippling side effects and a long recovery, so they wanted first to try an alternate route. More stents, beta blockers, statins—these were the words I'd heard thrown around over and over again. The doctors performed a couple more procedures on him, but each one left him lower, more lethargic, needing longer and longer to recover. The angioplasty—the surgical procedure that precedes the placement of a stent—required cutting opening a vein in his thigh, and the last time I'd seen him he'd been lying there with a sandbag on his lap, a necessary precaution to keep the wound from reopening. They'd been monitoring him for longer than was usual, keeping him in the hospital until his levels dropped below a certain number. His cholesterol was so high they were worried he'd have another heart attack.

This one, they said, might kill him.

I'd not doubted it would. I'd been waiting for that call, for the moment that would redefine my life, make sense of my brother's death, establish some kind of existential equilibrium. I'd been waiting for it, praying for it—

And now he was coming home.

I didn't know how to feel.

I didn't know that I wanted to feel anything at all.

I sighed as I turned over, pressed my cold face against the cold pillow. I was curled up like a fiddlehead, my frozen feet tucked against each other. No matter how hard I tried to create friction under the heavy covers, my body would not warm. I shivered, squeezed my eyes shut, listened to the faint ticking of the clock above my desk. Listened to my racing heart.

It had never stopped pounding.

My heart was still beating so hard it was beginning to scare me, beginning to hurt. It thudded dangerously in my chest even now, in the dead of night, made it somehow impossible to breathe. I did not know how to describe what I was feeling, what I was thinking. I'd been trying to disregard the entire night, trying to bury it the way I buried all else that troubled me, but this—somehow this was different. I had lost my head when my heart was most exposed, easily pierced. Recovery, I realized, would be slow.

I thought of God.

I had broken a rule by kissing Ali, had snapped in half a piece of dogma, kicked to the ground a religious guidepost. It wasn't the first time I'd done as much, and it certainly wouldn't be the last, but I was disconcerted nonetheless.

Even Mehdi, I knew, would've been stunned.

Mehdi was three years older than Ali, and the two of them had grazed each other's lives in the way those of their stratum did. Ali and Mehdi were that specific vintage of beautiful Muslim teenager who showed up at the mosque only occasionally, usually for major events and holidays, and often forced into attendance by their parents. They found religion equal parts compelling and ridiculous, and were generally uncertain about God. But it was precisely their lack of firm conviction that made it easier for them to assimilate—made it easier for them to belong to many groups, as opposed to one.

I'd always envied that kind of freedom. It would've been easier, I often thought, to have been exactly that variety of half-hearted Muslim, one who could more easily walk away from faith in order to be accepted.

What was it like? I wondered, to slough off this skin when convenient, to be looked upon by the world as something other than a cockroach. I feared I'd never know. I'd always carried with me a burden of conviction I could not set down. I could not deny the beliefs that shaped me any more than I could deny the color of my eyes.

It made for a lonely life.

There was no refuge for my brand of loneliness. I was neither Iranian enough to be accepted by Iranians, nor American enough to be accepted by my peers. I was neither religious enough for people at the mosque, nor secular enough for the rest of the world. I lived, always, on the uncertain plane of a hyphen.

I closed my eyes, took a deep breath.

Even now I could feel Ali's lips against my throat, could smell him as if he'd been trapped here, against my skin. My eyes flew open.

I had finally proven Zahra right.

I'd finally crossed the line she'd always feared I'd cross. I'd finally ceded control, given in to myself. I had no intention of telling anyone what happened between me and Ali tonight, but I pictured Zahra's face nonetheless, imagined her outrage.

For the very first time, I could not bring myself to care.

LAST YEAR

PART IV

It had been a strange, exhausting day. I'd woken up late, rushed to school, worn the wrong sweater, fought with my best friend, fumbled my way through classes. I'd started the day wrong and spent the rest of it trying to catch up, hoping to salvage what was left of the afternoon. And up until fifteen seconds ago, I thought I'd done just that. I thought I'd survived the worst of it. But now—now I wondered whether this day might kill me after all.

Can we talk?

I'd been staring at his message for the last fifteen seconds. I just stood there, frozen in the middle of my room, paralyzed by indecision.

Today, after months of tension, Zahra and I had finally

managed to find our way back to something like normal. Things had been shaky between us for so long—her mood swings were particularly hard to navigate—but I was beginning to hope we could fix things. Zahra had been, at times, shockingly cruel to me, but it wasn't difficult to forgive her lapses, especially not when I understood why she was struggling.

We were all struggling.

It was an awful time—politically and emotionally—for everyone in America, but there was a special pain in being made to feel like we weren't allowed to join in, like we had no right to mourn alongside our fellow citizens. American Muslims had a great deal to mourn—more than most people bothered to imagine. We were gutted not only by the horrible tragedy that had befallen our country, but by the disastrous fallout affecting our religious communities, and the personal losses we suffered—friends and family dead, missing—in the wars overseas. But none of that seemed to matter; no one wanted to hear about our pain.

Most days, I understood why. Some days, I wanted to scream.

It was a lonely, isolating time. I didn't want to lose Zahra; I knew too well how difficult it was to find a true friend, especially now.

But Ali was my friend, too.

I looked up then, looked out the window. My phone vibrated.

I can come by

Zahra was wrong. Her accusations were baseless. There was nothing going on between me and Ali, we had never hooked up, had never done anything inappropriate. But the truth didn't seem to matter. It had become increasingly clear to me that the only way to keep both siblings in my life was to keep Ali at a distance—a task proving harder to accomplish than I'd ever imagined. A low-voltage charge had existed between the two of us for as long as I'd been old enough to understand it, and some time last year that charge finally sparked, caught fire. I'd been trying desperately to ignore it. Ali had not.

Just for a few minutes? I wrote back.

Okay

Another buzz.

Same spot?

Guilt briefly seized my mind, paralyzed my fingers.

Twice. Twice we'd met up before. Only twice, and only in the last month, but somehow we'd already acquired a *spot*. Ali and I had spent a lot of time together over the years, but we'd never arranged it, never aligned our lives with the express purpose of being alone together. Not until he'd texted me that first time—

Can you come outside?

And I'd run out the door.

"What's going on?" I'd said, racing toward him. I was out of breath and confused, trying to read the look on his face. "Is everything okay?"

"Wow." Ali shook his head, smiled. "Okay, I didn't realize someone had to die in order for me to have a minute alone with you."

I'd gone suddenly, unearthly still. "What?"

"I just wanted to see you," he'd said. "Is that okay?"

"Oh." I could not seem to steady my breathing. "Oh."

He'd laughed.

"You just"—I frowned—"you mean you don't have anything important you need to tell me?"

He laughed again. "Not really."

"You just wanted to see me?"

He smiled at the sky. "Yeah."

"But we see each other every day."

Finally, he looked me in the eye. Took a deep breath. "Shadi."

"Yeah?"

He shoved his hands in his pockets, nodded toward the sidewalk. "Come on," he said quietly. "Walk with me."

That was the first time.

The second time—I had no good excuse for seeing him the second time. The second time was probably a mistake, the kind of decision born of simple, reflexive desire. I liked to tell myself that nothing happened, because nothing happened. I'd been doing homework while shaking a box of Nerds into my mouth when he texted me, so I closed my binder and tucked the box under my arm.

We went on another walk that day, passing the candy between us as we went. We didn't mean to go anywhere in particular, but ended up at the library near my house, which was where I always told my mom I was going anyway.

I quickly lost track of time. We were sitting on a bench outside the building, talking about all manner of nothing. At one point I laughed so hard at something he said I nearly choked to death on Nerds, after which I tried harder to be serious, an effort that only made me nervous—and that forced into stark relief the unnamed body of truth that sat between us.

Ali didn't mind the quiet.

He stared at me, unspeaking, and I felt it, felt everything he did not say. It was there in the way he breathed, in the way he shifted beside me, in the way his gaze dropped, briefly, to my lips. My hands trembled. I dropped the box of candy and its contents went flying across the street. My heart raced as I stared at the mess, at the pink and purple pebbles settling into cracks in the concrete. My every instinct was screaming at me, screaming that something was about to happen.

I'd just looked up at him when my phone rang.

It was my mom. My mom, who, after angrily pointing out that the sun was nearly gone from the sky, demanded I return home. I hung up and felt not unlike a dying light, flaring bright before burning out. I couldn't bring myself to meet Ali's eyes.

I didn't know what to say.

I'd never have said what I was really thinking, which was that I wanted to stay there, with him, forever. It was a shocking thought. Terrifying in scope, in the demands it placed upon our bodies. Somehow, he seemed to understand.

"Yeah," he said softly. "Me too."

I took a deep breath now, looked out the window again. My chest felt tight, like my heart was pushing, pulling, trying to escape. The mere sight of his name in my phone inspired in me a paroxysm of emotion I could not ignore. But one way or another, something always forced me to walk away from him, and I knew—knew, and didn't know how—that this, the third time, would be the last.

Yes, I typed back.
Same spot.

I stepped out into the light of a falling sun.

The weather had changed its mind again, the skies clearing, heating up in the second half of the day. It was an early evening in late September, the air warm and fragrant, the glow only just beginning to gild the streets. It was one of those rare golden hours, full of promise.

I'd been so certain of my commitment to see Ali for only a few minutes that I hadn't even told my parents I was leaving.

We lived in a safe, sleepy neighborhood—the kind of place you didn't drive through if you didn't live there—which meant that, for the most part, the streets were empty. Quiet.

I'd disappeared into the yard, slipped through the back gate; I figured I'd be back before anyone even noticed I was gone. I glanced at the sun as I walked, felt the wind shape itself around me. On days like this I imagined myself moving with grace, my body inspired into elegance by the breeze, the flattering light. Most of the time, this sort of quiet made me calm.

Today, I could hardly breathe.

I felt nothing but nerves as I neared the end of the street. I was trying, desperately, to steady my pounding heart, to kill the butterflies trapped between my ribs.

Ali was sitting on the curb.

He stood up when he saw me, stared at me until he was blinded by a shaft of golden light. He shielded his face with his forearm, turned his body away from the sun. For a moment, he looked like he'd been caught in a flame.

"Hey," I said quietly.

Ali said nothing at first, then took a sharp breath. "Hi," he said, and exhaled.

We found a patch of shade under a tree, stood in it. I looked at leaves, branches. Wondered how fast a heart could beat before it broke.

Ali was staring at a stop sign when he said, "Shadi, I can't do this anymore."

Impossibly, my heart found a way to beat faster.

"But we're not doing anything," I said.

He met my eyes. "I know."

I wanted to sit down. Lie down. My mind wasn't entirely certain what was happening, but my body—my faint, feverish body—had no doubt. Even my skin seemed to know. Every inch of me was taut with fear, with feeling. I had the strangest desire to find a shovel, to bury myself under the weight of it all.

Ali looked away then, made a sound, something like a laugh. Three times he opened his mouth to speak, and each time he came up short. Finally, he said—

"Please. Say something."

I was staring at him. I couldn't stop staring at him. "I can't."

"Why not?"

I was horrified to hear my voice shake when I said, "Because I'm scared."

He took a step closer. "Why are you scared?"

I whispered his name and it was practically a plea, a bid for mercy.

He said: "I keep waiting, Shadi. I keep waiting for this feeling to go away, but it's just getting worse. Sometimes I feel like it's actually killing me."

He laughed. I couldn't breathe.

"Isn't that strange?" he said. I saw the tremble in his hands before he pushed them through his hair. "I thought this sort of thing was supposed to make people happy."

Something unlocked my tongue then. Unlocked my bones.

"What sort of thing?"

He turned to face me, his arms dropping to his sides. "You know, I don't even think I know exactly when I fell in love with you. It was years ago."

I thought, for a moment, that my feet might be sinking into the earth. I looked down, looked back up, heard my heart beating. I took an unconscious step backward and nearly stumbled over the base of a nearby tree, its overgrown roots.

"Shadi, I love you," he said, stepping closer. "I've always loved you—"

"Ali, please." My eyes were filling with tears. I couldn't stop shaking my head. "Please. Please. I can't do this."

He was silent for so long it almost scared me. I watched him swallow. I saw him struggle to collect himself, his thoughts—and then, quietly—

"You can't do what?"

"I can't do this to her. To Zahra."

Something flickered in his eyes then. Surprise. Confusion. "You can't do what to Zahra?"

"This, *this*—"

"What's *this*, Shadi?" He closed the remaining distance between us and suddenly he was right in front of me, suddenly I couldn't think straight.

My heart seemed to be screaming, pounding fists against my chest. I wanted desperately to touch him, to tell him the truth, to admit that I fell asleep most nights thinking about him, that I found his face in nearly all my favorite memories.

But I didn't.

Couldn't.

The sun was streaking across the sky, painting his face in ethereal ribbons of color, blurring the edges of everything. I felt like we were disappearing.

I couldn't help it when I whispered, "You look like a Renoir painting right now."

He blinked. "What?"

"I'm sorry, I don't know why I—"

"Shadi—"

"Please," I said, cutting him off. My voice was breaking. "Please don't make me do this."

"I'm not making you do anything."

"You are. You're making me choose between you and Zahra, and I can't. You know I can't. It's not a fair fight."

Ali shook his head. "Why would you have to choose? This has nothing to do with my sister."

"It has everything to do with your sister," I said desperately. "She's my best friend. This—us—it would ruin my relationship with her. It would ruin *your* relationship with her."

"What? How? What would we be doing wrong?"

"You don't understand," I said. "It's complicated—she—"

"God," he cried, turning away. "I fucking hate my sister."

I felt the fight leave me then. Felt the emotion drain from my body. "Ali. This is the problem. This is the whole problem."

He spun back around. "For the love of God, Shadi, just tell me what *you* want. Do you want me? Do you want to be with me? Because if you do, that's all that matters. We can figure out everything else."

"We can't," I said. "It's not that simple."

He was shaking his head. "It is that simple. I need it to be that simple. Because I can't do this anymore. I can't take it anymore. I can't see you every day and just pretend this isn't killing me."

"You have to."

He went suddenly still. I watched it happen, watched him stiffen, then straighten, in real time. And then, two words, so raw they might've been ripped out of his chest:

"I can't."

I thought I might actually lose my head then, thought I might start crying, or worse, kiss him, and instead I racked my mind for an answer, for a solution to this madness, and seized upon the first stupid thought that entered my head. I spoke recklessly, hastily, before I'd even had a chance to think it through.

"Then maybe—maybe it would be better if we didn't see each other. Maybe we just shouldn't be in each other's lives anymore."

Ali recoiled, stepping back as if he'd been struck. He waited for what seemed an eternity for me to speak, to take it back, but my lips had gone numb, my mind too stupid to navigate this labyrinth of emotion. I did not know what I'd just done.

Finally—without a word—Ali walked away. Disappeared into the dying sunset.

I realized, as I cried myself to sleep that night, that I might've hurt him less had I simply driven a stake through his heart.

DECEMBER

2003

SEVENTEEN

I kicked off the covers, dragged myself out of bed.

I couldn't sleep, likely wouldn't sleep with this pounding, tangled mess of a head, heart. I wrapped myself in my blanket, quietly opened my bedroom door, and padded downstairs. All the bedrooms were on the same floor, which left the living room fair game at night.

Once downstairs, I switched on a light.

The scene flickered to life, the unbroken hum of electricity filling me with a vague sadness. Dining room, kitchen, living room. It all felt cold without my mother in it. I collapsed onto the couch and burrowed into my blanket, hoping to numb my mind with a reliable opiate.

I turned on the television, was not rewarded.

Flashing banners across the bottom of the screen read *BREAKING NEWS*, a scrolling marquee neatly summarizing the storms I would weather at school for the next six weeks. Right now the news anchors were discussing the possibility of other undercover Al Qaeda members living here, in America, new data suggesting that they'd slipped into the country around the same time as the 9/11 hijackers. We were currently searching for them.

I turned off the television.

The FBI had been cold-calling members of our congregation recently, interrogating them over the phone and terrifying them witless. So many people had been assigned an agent that, for some people, it had become kind of a running joke.

I didn't find it funny.

The random interrogations were creating division, causing people to question and distrust each other. The Muslim community had never been perfect—we'd always had our weirdos and our disagreements and a spiny generation of racist, sexist elders far too attached to culture and tradition to see things clearly—

But we had so much more than that, too.

We fed the poor, volunteered endlessly, organized peace dialogues, took in refugees. Nearly all the kids at the mosque had been born to parents who'd fled war in another country, or else came here to find better and safer opportunities for their families. We'd built a sanctuary together, a safe house for the otherwise marginalized. I loved our mosque. Loved gathering there for prayers and holidays and holy months.

But things were changing.

The FBI wasn't just interrogating people—they were also looking for recruits within the congregation. They were offering large sums of money to anyone willing to spy on their friends and family. We knew this because people shared their horror stories after prayers, stood near the exit wearing only one shoe, gesticulating wildly with the other. What we didn't know, of course, was who had turned. We didn't know who among us had accepted the paycheck, and as a result, we were poised to devour ourselves alive.

The thought made me hungry.

I made myself a bowl of cereal, sat under dim light at the kitchen table. There was once a time when my parents kept the kitchen fully stocked, when meals were a gathering time, when food was the great smoother of troubles, delicious and plentiful. These days when I opened the fridge I found milk and wrinkled cucumbers and a carton of eggs. In the pantry we had little but canned tomato paste, a box of cereal, dried herbs, and Top Ramen—a perfect recipe for our electric stove that was only any good at boiling water.

I listened to the lights hum.

I took another bite of cold cereal, shivering as I tried again to remember where I'd left my phone. It had been easier than I'd expected to go so long without it; I'd little use for it without Zahra in my life. Other than her, my brother was the only one who ever contacted me. My heart leaped at that thought, tried to wrench loose my emotional control, but I forced down another spoonful of Cheerios and compelled myself to think, instead, about not choking. And perhaps about homework. I had endless amounts of homework.

I had been unwilling to look too closely at my recent failures.

Failure number one: I missed my multivariable calculus class last night, which meant that even perfect scores across the board would get me no more than a B. This seemed an unbelievable, riotous injustice, and though it occurred to me that I could probably explain to the teacher that my mother had been in the hospital, the slim chance that he might not believe me—or worse, ask for proof of my mother's mental breakdown—was motivation enough for me to remain silent.

Failure number two: I'd failed my AP Art History exam today. I didn't need to wait for the results to know this truth. I'd turned in a blank exam; I was going to fail it. Still, there was a chance it might not weigh as heavily, in the end. My teacher was the kind who liked to make the final exam worth half our grade, and as we'd just entered the second week of December, my last chance was right around the corner. In fact, in a couple of weeks I'd have to survive a deluge of examinations, and I had no idea how I'd catch up. There was still so much more looming—college applications, for example.

College applications.

I inhaled so suddenly I coughed, milk and half a Cheerio

having gone down the wrong pipe. What was I thinking? I wasn't going away for college. My eyes teared and I wiped at them with my sleeve, covering my mouth as I continued to cough.

Was I going away for college?

Could I abandon my mother here? All this time I'd been waiting for my father to die, I'd also been considering my future. Shayda was well on her way to transferring elsewhere, to getting married. With three of the five of us gone, I didn't think I'd have the heart to leave my mother behind.

But now—

A shoot of hope pushed up through my rotting ribs. The one fringe benefit of my father not dying: I might be able to go away.

Start over somewhere else.

When the phone rang I startled so badly I spilled cereal all over myself. I stood up, felt scattered, reached for a towel. I mopped myself up as best I could, sighed over the state of my blanket, glanced at the clock. It was nearly midnight, far too late for friendly calls.

Fear shot through me as I lifted the receiver.

"Hello?" I said.

A beat.

"Hello?" I tried again.

"Babajoon, toh ee?"

My already erratic heart rate spiked. *Babajoon* was a term of endearment—it literally meant *Father's dear*—and hearing it without warning, hearing it in my father's unexpectedly tender voice—

I lost my composure.

I took a deep breath, forced a smile on my face.

"Salam, Baba," I said. "Khoobeen shoma?" So formal. I always used formal pronouns and conjugations with my father, even to say *Are you well?*

"Alhamdullilah. Alhamdullilah."

He didn't say yes. He didn't say he was fine. He said, *Thank God, thank God,* which could mean any number of things.

"What are you doing awake so late?" he said in Farsi. "Don't you have school tomorrow? I can't remember what day it is."

I held steady as my heart sustained a hairline fracture.

How long had he been in the hospital, drugged and dissected, that he couldn't remember what day it was?

"Yes," I said. "I do have school tomorrow. I just couldn't sleep."

He laughed. The fracture deepened.

"Me neither," he said softly. Sighed. "I miss you all so much."

I clenched the phone desperately. "Maman said you're coming home tomorrow. She said you're doing better."

He went quiet.

"Mamanet khabeedeh?" *Is your mother asleep?*

"Yes," I said, my eyes burning, threatening. "Why? What's wrong?"

"Hichi, azizam. Hichi." *Nothing, my love. Nothing.*

He was lying.

"Baba?" I was holding the phone with two hands now. "Are you coming home tomorrow?"

"I don't know," he said in English. "I don't know."

"But—"

"Babajoonam, could you wake your mother for me?" Back to Farsi.

"Yes," I said quickly. "Yes, of course. I'll—"

"It's so good to hear your voice," he said, sounding suddenly faraway. Tired. "I haven't seen you lately. You've been busy? How's Zahra?"

My eyes were filling with tears, my traitorous heart tearing apart. My father was dying. My father was dying and I had not been to visit him, had not wanted to talk to him, had delighted in planning his funeral. I suddenly hated myself with a violence I could not articulate, with a passion that nearly took my breath away.

"Yes," I said shakily. "Zahra's good. She—"

"Khaylee dooset daram, Shadi joon. Midooni? Khaylee ziad. Mikhastam faghat bedooni." *I love you, Shadi dear. Did you know? Very much. I just wanted you to know.*

Tears spilled down my cheeks and I held the phone to my chest, gasped back a sudden sob, pressed my fist to my mouth.

My father did not talk like this. He never talked like this. I'd never doubted that he loved me, but he'd never said it out loud. Never, not once in my entire life.

"Shadi? Rafti?" *Did you leave?*

I heard his voice, small and staticky, the speaker muffled against my shirt. I brought the phone back to my ear, took a breath, then another.

"I love you, too, Baba."

"Geryeh nakon, azizam. Geryeh nakon." *Don't cry, my love. Don't cry.* "Everything will be okay."

"I'll go get Maman," I said, eyes welling, hands trembling. I no longer trusted myself, no longer understood my mercurial heart. "I'll be right back."

EIGHTEEN

At dawn, I broke down my mother's door.

I'd never gone back to sleep. I'd run up the stairs with the cordless phone, woken my mom as gently as possible, and, once I'd pressed the receiver into her hands, tiptoed back outside to wait. I stood in the shadows, held my breath. I was waiting for her to emerge, waiting for news about my father.

She never came out.

Instead, my mother had been crying for hours, the muted, muffled sounds no more easily ignored than a piercing scream. I felt close to vomiting as I sat in the hall outside her bedroom, sat in the dark like a dead spider, arms wrapped around legs crossed and bent at the knees. I held myself as I shivered, shivered as I waited, waited for it to stop, for her to stop crying, to go back to bed. I waited so long I heard the whine of a hinge, a soft close. I felt Shayda move down the hall, felt her warmth as she sat next to me. Our shoulders touched. She didn't flinch.

We didn't speak.

I'd knocked on my mother's door a hundred times, rattled the handle to no response. I stood again and pounded on it now, shouted for her to open the door. Only once, weakly, did she respond.

"Please, azizam," she said. "I just want to be alone."

The sun was coming up over the horizon, splintering the world in blinding strokes of color, painting the white walls of our house with a terrible, morbid beauty.

I left.

I ran down the stairs, ignoring Shayda's sharp, relentless questions. I slammed open the connecting door to the garage, rifled through my father's toolbox, retrieved a hammer, and charged back up the stairs, recognizing my mania only in Shayda's horrified face. I didn't care. I couldn't take it anymore, not now that I knew, not now that I knew what my mother was doing, why she was hiding.

I couldn't just stand here and let it happen.

Shayda looked at me like I was crazy, tried to yank the hammer out of my hand. She insisted that our mother deserved her privacy.

"She's upset," Shayda said, more gently than I knew her capable. "She'd gotten her hopes up about Baba. She'll be okay in the morning."

"Shayda," I said, flexing my fingers around the hilt. "It *is* morning."

"This is wrong. Maman has the right to be left alone. Sometimes it's good to cry—maybe it'll make her feel better."

I looked her in the eye. "You don't understand."

"Shadi, stop—"

"Go back to bed," I barked at my older sister.

Her eyes widened. "Oh my God. You really have lost your mind."

I swung the hammer.

Shayda screamed. I swung it again, three more times, shattered the cheap metal knob, splintered the thin wood. I kicked the door, slammed it open with my shoulder.

I tossed the tool to the carpet, found my mother in her bathroom.

She was sitting on the cold tile in a robe, her bare legs stretched out in front of her. She was staring at the ground like a broken doll, her neck limp, a pair of open cuticle scissors clenched in one hand.

I saw the marks on her shins, the cuts that scored the skin but had not yet split. She was not bleeding.

"Maman," I breathed.

When she looked up, she looked no older than me. Terrified, shame-faced. Alone. Tears had stained her cheeks, her clothes.

"I couldn't do it," she said in Farsi, her voice breaking. "I didn't do it. I couldn't do it."

I dropped to my knees in front of her. Took her hand. Pried the cuticle scissors from her fingers, tossed them aside.

"I kept thinking of you, and your sister," she was saying, tears falling fast down her face. "I couldn't do it."

I lifted her up, braced her head against my chest as she shattered in my arms. Her cries were desperate, ragged, gut-wrenching sobs. She clung to me like a child, wept like a baby.

"It's going to be okay," I whispered. "You're going to be okay."

I felt, but did not hear, a soundless movement. I turned my head carefully, slowly so my mother wouldn't notice. Shayda was standing in the broken doorway, staring at the scene in a state of paralyzing disbelief. I felt true love for her in that moment, felt our souls solder together, knew our lives would be forever forged by a similar pain.

We locked eyes.

She covered her mouth with her hands, shook her head. She was gone before her tears made a sound.

My mother went to work an hour later. Shayda and I went to our respective schools. For all the world we were your garden variety of incomprehensible Muslim, one-note and easily caricatured. We articulated limbs, moved our lips to make sounds, smiled at customers, said hello to teachers.

The world continued to spin, taking with it, my mind.

I felt true delirium as I moved, exhaustion unlike any I'd ever known. I couldn't even fathom how I was still upright; I felt like I was hearing everything from far away, felt like my body was not my own. My mind had the processing speed of molasses, my eyes blurring constantly. I needed to find a way to focus, needed to remember how to pay attention. I had failed, once again, to complete any of the homework due today, and I felt shame as I watched other students turn in their essays and worksheets, raise their hands to answer questions in clear and focused sentences. This month was suddenly more critical than ever and I was drowning, drowning when I needed, desperately, to keep my head above water.

As long as my father stayed alive, I planned on going away to college. I didn't want to stay here, spend two years at the community college, transfer eventually. I wanted to leave as soon as possible. I wanted to leave and maybe never, ever come back. And I wanted to get into a good school.

I nearly screamed at the sound of a gunshot.

I sat up suddenly, hyperventilating, heart racing in my chest. I heard a roar of laughter, looked up, looked around, realized I'd fallen asleep. My seat was in the far right corner of this class, but it was in the first row, and my AP Chemistry teacher, Mr. Mathis, was standing in front of my desk now, arms crossed, shaking his head. At his feet was a massive textbook—a textbook, I realized, he'd dropped on purpose.

It was a cruel joke.

I felt my face flush, heat jolting through my body. People were still laughing. I sat up in my seat, kept my eyes on my desk. I wanted to turn my skin inside out.

"I'm sorry," I said quietly.

"You want to stay out late? That's not my problem," Mr.

Mathis said sharply. "Get your sleep at home. Not in my class."

"Of course. I'm sorry."

He shot me a dark look. Carried on with his lecture. I spent the rest of the period staring at the textbook at my feet, feeling as though all the blood had drained from my body, pooled onto the floor.

My father was not coming home today.

He was not dying just yet, but he was also not coming home today, and that was all I really understood at the moment. My mom hadn't talked much, hadn't explained more than was absolutely necessary, and flatly refused my suggestion that she go to a support group for grieving parents. She'd audibly gasped when I proposed she see a therapist. She'd looked so outraged I actually panicked; I thought for a moment she might never speak to me again. But then she ate the eggs I made her for breakfast.

Something had changed between us that morning, and I still didn't know what it was, had not yet figured out how to define it. But I could tell, just by looking into her eyes, that my mother had unclenched an iota. She seemed relieved—relieved, perhaps, to no longer be living with such a crushing secret.

"I'll be okay," she kept saying. "I'll be fine."

I did not believe her.

I spent my lunch period sleeping at a table in the library, head bowed over my folded arms. I felt like I'd only just closed my eyes when someone shook my shoulder, rattled my skeleton back to life. I awoke suddenly, my nerves fraying in an instant.

When I looked up, I saw a blur of color. Eyes. Mouth.

"Noah."

"Hey," he said, but he was frowning. "Are you okay? The bell just rang."

"Oh." I tried to stand, but the action proved harder to accomplish than I'd expected. "What—what are you doing here?"

"We were supposed to have lunch together, remember?" He suddenly smiled. "I brought a newspaper and everything. But your friend Yumiko told me you'd bailed on her for the library."

I frowned. Dimly, I remembered running into her, telling her I'd be in the library for lunch. That conversation felt like it'd happened a lifetime ago. "You brought a newspaper?"

Noah smiled wider. "Yeah."

I laughed, collected my things in a daze, moved through the room with a pronounced slowness. I wanted to say, *That's so nice*, but it seemed like too much work.

"Hey—what's wrong? Are you sick?" I heard his voice, heard it like it was coming from the stars.

I shook my head, the single motion disorienting me. I tried to say *I'm just tired*, but I wasn't sure it went through. My feet moved even more stupidly than my mind and I suddenly tripped over my own shoes, caught myself against a research table, the sharp edge slamming into my gut. I gasped as I steadied myself, caught my breath.

I looked up, stared at the exit, wondered why the end always seemed so far away.

Someone touched me.

I turned my head as if through panes of glass, sounds shattering against my face. Noah. Noah was here, his hand on my arm, his head bent toward my face, he said, "Shadi," he said, "are you okay?" and I heard his voice like I pictured sound—slow and loud, reverberating.

I saw color, flashes of it.

Are you? he said. Okay?

Are you Do you need to see do you need the the nursedoyou okay maybe see the go, go home home?

I felt it, when I fell.

I heard someone shout, I felt something soft—warm arms, a gentle landing—a gasp, rough carpet under my face, my eyes closing. I heard sound, so much sound, loud and round, shuddering. I tried to pry open my eyes. They refused.

My lips, on the other hand, acquiesced.

"Please." My mouth moved against commercial carpeting, my nose filled with dust. I felt everything move, felt my body spin.

Someone was talking to me. Hands on my back.

"Please," I whispered. "Don't let them call my mother. She's not— She— *Please*," I said, felt myself drifting.

I didn't know whether I was dreaming.

Don't let them call my mother, I tried to say. Tried to scream it. *Please—*

NINETEEN

Zahra had redecorated.

I stared first at her ceiling, the smooth white skin blemished by neither light fixture nor popcorn, no cobwebs to be seen. I turned my head a single micrometer in this grave of pillows and saw her new desk atop which sat her new computer, a stack of makeup and books, a small mirror. I saw a new lamp—still lit—standing in a corner. I saw the same laundry basket, the same six hooks on the wall from which hung a dozen purses. A single tennis shoe was pushing free of her closet door, the handle of which was hung with an ornament of the evil eye.

I'd made a huge mistake.

I tried, but could not move my arms, not yet. I felt thick with weight, forgotten under setting concrete. I tore open my mouth, wet my lips, remembered I had teeth.

I did not know how long I'd been sleeping, but a single

glance out Zahra's darkened window was enough to awaken my fear. I sat straight up and regretted it, felt my head fissure with pain.

I pushed myself to my feet, felt a familiar scrape against my ribs. I reached under my shirt to retrieve today's newspaper from my waistband and promptly tossed the paper in Zahra's trash. The sight inspired in me a flicker of memory.

Noah.

I vaguely remembered sitting in the nurse's office. I vaguely remembered that Noah came with me, that he half carried me there. *He'd brought a newspaper.* The thought almost made me smile. It was a strange silver lining in all this chaos to think that I'd somehow managed to make a new friend, that the rest of the school year might be a little less lonely. But then I remembered the sound of my own voice begging, begging them even as I sat in a hard, wooden chair with my eyes closed, to spare my mother the phone call.

I'd not thought this through.

Please don't call my mother was all I'd had, my sole functioning brain cell screaming out a single directive.

I'd not thought about who they might call instead.

My father was in the hospital. Shayda was not listed as one of my emergency contacts. But I still remember the form Zahra's dad had to fill out the day he came to get me, just three months ago.

Zahra's parents were in my file.

I stood stock-still in my ex—best friend's bedroom and

stared at myself in her mirror, the mirror above her dresser, the one she'd had for as long as I'd known her. I took in my strange, ghostly appearance, the blush-colored silk scarf tied loosely at my throat, half-fallen off my head. My dark hair was coming loose, my normally pale skin now pink with heat, with the flush of fresh sleep. My eyes were the bright, strange green of a person on drugs.

I looked slow, soft, newly cooked.

It was how I felt, too.

Zahra must've known I was here. Zahra—who'd accused me of being a calculating opportunist, who'd warned me to stay the hell away from her family—had to have known that I'd been asleep in her beautiful, soft bed, and she had to have hated it, hated me for it, for forcing her to play nice at what was no doubt her parents' behest. The thought made me suddenly sick. I didn't know whether it was even possible to escape the mortification of such a scene. I thought it might inhale me.

I glanced at the clock on the wall and was comforted, for a moment, by the knowledge that Zahra was in class at the community college right now. It was Wednesday night, the night I, too, was supposed to be in class at the community college. This was the third time I'd missed my multivariable calculus class, which meant that even with perfect scores, my best possible grade had now dropped to a C.

The realization struck me like a blow.

I'd never gotten a C in anything before. Worse, that C was contingent upon flawless work in all other areas. But

I'd already missed three days; I'd already missed homework, would struggle to catch up for exams. I'd more than likely end up with a D, which was considered failing. I'd have to retake the class. I didn't even know if they'd let me retake the class.

I stared at a single thing as my heart raced: a plush pink teddy bear perched in an armchair beside Zahra's bed. I stared at its big glass eyes, at the tiny red heart stitched onto its white belly. I did not own any stuffed animals. My father had gotten rid of mine when I was twelve; he'd taken my childhood things to Goodwill while I was at school. When I'd cried, he'd told me it was time to grow up.

Zahra would have all that I only ever dreamed of: the necessary love and stability to survive this life with grace, and the parental support required to be the dutiful, promising student I'd tried and failed to be.

I took a ragged breath. Clasped my shaking hands.

I had another hour before Zahra's class ended, and I thought I might escape before then, find somewhere to kill time until I could walk home at my normal hour, pretend everything was as it should be.

I stepped into the adjoining bathroom, apologizing to Zahra's ghost as I borrowed her toothpaste, finger-brushed my teeth, rinsed my mouth. I splashed cold water on my face, but my cheeks would not cool. I looked overheated to the extreme, my lips brighter, redder than usual, everything hot to the touch.

I shivered, suddenly.

I readjusted my scarf, tried to contain my slippery straight hair, but I'd lost a couple of the bobby pins that held my longer bangs in place, and dark strands kept coming loose. I stared, longingly, at some of Zahra's hair clips, and tried to decide whether it would be truly reprehensible to take them without her permission. I picked them up. Weighed them in my hands. We had such a long, storied history that I didn't think she'd begrudge me something so small.

But then I remembered, with a sinking sensation, that she'd been unwilling to offer me even a ride in the pouring rain. We'd both been headed to the same destination—her, in a warm, dry car; me, caught in a deluge without an umbrella.

I dropped the pins back on her counter.

When I turned around, I collided with a wall of heat.

I knew, I knew, I'd known he might be here but I'd not allowed myself to think about it, could not bring myself to process the possibility of so much humiliation. This was not how I wanted to see Ali again. Not like this, not trapped inside his sister's bedroom after a delirious collapse, not saved by his parents because I had no one of my own to call. I knew how I presented, could see how his family must see me, with pity, with pity and charity, an aching sadness in their eyes that tore me in half.

This was not what I wanted.

My heart pounded dangerously as I looked up at him. He wasn't supposed to be here. It broke the rules of basic propriety for him to have entered his sister's bedroom while I slept. I was a guest in his home, a guest who'd not given him permission to enter, and we both knew it. I didn't need to say it. I could tell by the frightened look on his face that he knew he'd taken a risk, one that might end in disaster.

"Hey," he said. He took a deep breath, gave it back.

He had the darkest eyes. Thick, inky lashes. There was a depth in his gaze, a collapsed star that beckoned, tempted me to peer inside, lose myself, and if not there—here, in the elegant lines of his face, in the sharpness of his jaw, in his smooth, dusky skin. There was so much to appreciate, so much for the eyes to enjoy.

But I, I could not stop staring at his mouth.

"Hi," I whispered.

"Hi," he said.

"You really shouldn't be here."

"I know. I'm sorry. I just—" He cut himself off. Did not continue.

I nodded for no reason. I stared at my socked feet, wondered who'd removed my shoes.

"I called you," he said quietly. "Last night." He laughed, then. Sighed. Turned away.

"I lost my phone."

He looked up. "Oh."

When I said nothing he exhaled, pushed a hand through his hair. It was a nervous habit, something he did a lot. I'd watched him do it for years, and I watched him do it now. I'd often wondered what it would feel like to touch him like that. His hair looked so soft.

"Shadi," he said. "What's going on?"

I dragged my eyes back to his face. "What do you mean?"

He froze at that, froze with something like anger. "What do you mean, *what do I mean*? You collapsed at school."

"Right. Yeah. Yes," I said. My heart was suddenly pounding again.

"Shadi."

I met his eyes. I saw the effort he was making to breathe, could see his chest moving, even out of focus. He was struggling to contain his frustration.

"What happened? The school told my parents you'd begged them not to call your own mom. Is that true?"

"Yes," I whispered.

"Why?"

I shook my head, looked away, bit my lip too hard. I was desperate to confess, to say nothing. I didn't know what to do; I only knew what my parents would want me to do, which was to protect their secrets, to protect their pain from public viewing.

So I said nothing. I stared at his chest and said nothing.

"You've been asleep here for the last four hours," he said quietly. "And no one knows what's going on."

"I'm sorry. I'm going to leave. I was going to leave before y—"

"Stop," he said angrily. "*Stop*. Just stop, okay? I've been trying to let this go, I've been trying not to push you to explain yourself, but I can't take it anymore. I can't. You have to tell me what's happening, Shadi, because you're starting to scare the shit out of me. Every single time I see you lately you're crying or injured or completely out of your mind and I ca—"

"I've never been out of my mind."

His eyebrows flew up. "You ran into the middle of a car accident! Tried to pull someone out of a damaged vehicle!"

"Oh." I'd forgotten about that.

"Yeah. Did you forget?" He smiled, but his eyes were angry. "Did you also forget when you nearly broke your skull? Is that why you never mentioned it again? You got that phone call about your mom and I drove you to the hospital and I didn't even ask you to explain—but I did think that, maybe, considering the fact that I had to get four stitches in my arm after catching your head on the pavement—"

"You had to get stitches? I didn't—"

"Yes, I had to get stitches, and I lied for you, lied to my parents and told them I'd ripped my arm open playing soccer because I didn't think you wanted people to know what was happening, but I thought you might at least tell *me* why your mom was in the hospital or why you fainted, but you never did, and still I let it go, told myself it was none of my business. And then, the next day, after you're done pretending to be a paramedic—"

"Ali—I'm sorry, I'm so sorry about your arm—"

"—you tell me everything is great, that your mom is waiting for you at home, and I knew you were lying—I knew it, I could just tell, it was written all over your face—but

I told myself to let it go, told myself not to pry—"

"Ali. *Please.*"

"And then," he said, breathing hard, dragging both hands down his face. "And then, God, and then—last night. Fucking last night, Shadi."

"Ali—"

"Stop saying my name like that. Don't—"

"*Ali*—"

"You're killing me," he said, his voice breaking. "What is happening? What are you doing to me? I used to have a life, I swear, three days ago I had a good life, Shadi, I'd moved on, I'd finally moved on after you tore my heart out of my fucking chest and now, now I'm— I don't know what I am."

"I'm sorry."

"Stop," he said desperately. "Stop saying you're sorry. Stop standing there looking at me like that. I can't take it, okay? I can't—"

"Ali, just let me say something— I just want t—"

The words died in my throat.

He'd walked away without warning, sat down heavily on Zahra's bed. "Please," he said, gesturing at me. "By all means, say something. For the love of God, say something."

I stared at him then, lost my nerve. Words jammed in my chest, inside my mouth. My excuses vanished, the day's events momentarily forgotten. I studied the tension in his shoulders; caught the tremble in his fingers before he curled them into fists.

I looked into his dark eyes and thought only one thing.

"I'm sorry."

"*Jesus.*" He dropped his head in his hands. "Why do you keep apologizing?"

"Because," I said. "Because I never did."

Ali's head lifted slowly, his spine straightened slowly. He unfurled before my eyes, turning toward me not unlike a bloom in search of the sun.

"I never wanted to hurt you," I whispered. "I'm so sorry I hurt you."

He went deathly still.

He stared at me now with a strange terror, stared at me like I might be about to kill him. "What are you talking about?"

"Us," I said. "You." I shook my head, felt close to tears. "I thought I was doing the right thing. I need you to know I thought I was doing the right thing. But I was sorry the moment I said it. I've been sorry every day since."

Ali got to his feet.

He became larger than life then, tall and stunning and real and he walked right up to me, was now standing right in front of me and I stepped back, felt my shoulders nudge open Zahra's bathroom door.

Ali was breathing hard. "What does that mean?"

I looked up at him, felt my world collapse.

We were now standing in Zahra's bathroom—*we were standing in Zahra's bathroom*—and there wasn't enough space between our bodies to lift a finger. My head was filling with steam, my thoughts evaporating.

"Ali, I don't— You're too close. I can't talk to you when you're this close to me. I can't even breathe when y—"

I gasped when he leaned in, pressed his forehead to mine. His hands were at my waist now, reeling me in, and I sank against his body with a sound, a kind of surrender.

He said nothing for what seemed like an eternity.

I listened to our hearts race, felt my skin heat. I felt desperate for something I could not articulate, for a need I could not fathom. We were standing this close and still light-years from where I wanted to be.

Ali closed his eyes.

My hands were on his chest. They'd landed there and I'd left them there and I loved the feel of him, his heat, this racing heartbeat under my hands that proved he was real, that this moment was real. Slowly, I dragged my hands down his chest, down the hard lines of his torso. I heard his sharp intake of breath, felt a tremor move through him, through me.

We both went suddenly still.

I was staring at his throat, the soft line of his neck, the hint of his collarbone. I watched him swallow. His hands tightened around my waist.

I looked up.

He said nothing but my name before he kissed me.

It was heat, a blistering sun, a pleasure so potent it felt closer to pain. I didn't know how but my back was suddenly against a wall, my bones trembling under the weight of him, his body pressed so hard against mine I thought it might leave an impression. He touched me desperately, dragged his hands up my body, braced my face as he broke me open. His lips were so soft against mine, against my cheeks, the tender skin beneath my jaw. I tried to hold on—pushing myself up on tiptoe, twining my arms around his neck—but he froze, suddenly, when my body moved against his, our jagged edges catching, tectonic plates striking. He stilled and seemed to stop breathing, our bodies fusing together.

Tentatively, I pushed my fingers through his hair. He thawed by degrees, his eyes closing, his breathing ragged as I drew my hands away from his head, trailed my fingers down his neck, pressed closer. Gently, I kissed the column of his throat, tasting salt and heat over and over until he made a sound, something desperate, something that shot pleasure through my body even as he tore away, took a step back. He dropped his face into trembling hands, let them fall to his sides. He looked into my eyes with a depth of emotion that nearly split me in half.

I felt like I might sink into the ground.

Two sharp knocks at Zahra's door and I straightened, we both stiffened. The real world came hurtling back into focus with stunning, sobering speed and I didn't even think, I just ran past him, closed the bathroom door behind me, shut him inside.

I had to lean against the wall to catch my breath, steady my head. My heart was pounding dangerously in my chest and

I closed my eyes, gave myself two more seconds to pull myself together before I headed for the door, glancing in the mirror as I went.

I froze.

Horror, horror at the state of my face, my appearance in general. I was flushed beyond reason, my eyes dilated with pleasure. Desire.

I was losing control. Losing my head.

I was certain now that I was probably going straight to hell for a myriad of reasons, not the least of which was my virulent desire for my father's death, and now this—this—

I spun around, took it all in.

Zahra's bedroom. I'd kissed Ali in her own bedroom. Any ancient sense of honor I'd once had compelled me now to recoil with shame. I was not proud of myself. I hadn't meant for any of this to happen. This, here, today, just now—I'd crossed a line, turned my back on the ghost of my best friend. Even after all this time, after all her cruelty, I felt punctured by sorrow. I'd wanted so much more for us.

But then—even as I felt the cold lash of guilt cool my feverish skin, I grew tired. Tired of this feeling, tired of owing Zahra a tithe of my happiness. My guilt was tempered by a realization, an awareness that nothing I'd ever done had been enough for her. I knew that for certain now. So many times I felt like I'd been strapped to the tracks of our friendship, Zahra the train that repeatedly ran me over, only to later complain that my body had broken her axles.

I was tired of it.

I'd been ashamed of myself for a number of things lately, but Zahra's unfair judgments were no longer among them. I would never again let her hold my feelings hostage. I would never again let her dictate the terms of my life.

Another sharp knock at the door and I startled.

Steadied.

It was time, I realized, to close the book of our friendship.

TWENTY

I nearly gasped when I saw her face.

I looked into her eyes—Zahra's mom's eyes—and my heart steadied on its own, my fears disappeared, my face blossomed into a familiar smile. I'd missed her, missed her face. A sudden, cold pain pierced through me.

Fereshteh khanoom, I called her.

Khanoom meant *lady*; it was an affectionate term, respectful. But her name, Fereshteh, meant *angel*.

"Bidari, khoshgelam?" She smiled. *Are you awake, my beauty?*

She opened her arms to me and I stepped into her hug, held on. She smelled the same, the way she always did, like rose water.

I pulled back, feeling suddenly young.

"Chetori?" she said. *How are you?* "Khoob khabeedi?" *Did you sleep well?*

223

"Thank you, yes," I said quietly. "Thank you for everything."

She beamed. "Asslan harfesham nazan," she said, dismissing my statement with a flutter of her fingers.

She was still wearing her hijab, and seemed to realize it as she spoke. In a single motion she slipped it off her head, explained with a laugh that she'd gotten home from work not long ago, had forgotten to take it off. She'd gotten home late, I realized. She'd probably stayed later than usual at the office, no doubt to make up for the time she'd lost in the middle of the day.

My smile felt suddenly weak.

"Bea bereem paeen," she said, not missing a beat. "Ghaza hazereh." *Let's go downstairs. Food is ready.*

"Oh, no," I said, panicked. "I can't— I should get home."

She laughed at me. Laughed and took me by the arm and literally dragged me down the stairs. My heart was pounding, my fear spiking.

"Please, Fereshteh khanoom. Lotf dareen, shoma." *You are very kind.* In Farsi, I said, "But I swear to God I'm not just trying to be polite. You've embarrassed me with your kindness."

I was laying it on thick with some old-school, effusive statements, but I did it on purpose. Iranian parents always seemed delighted when I talked like that, when I made the effort to be formal and polite. They found my incompetent Farsi oddly charming, especially with my American accent.

And just then, I did not disappoint.

Fereshteh khanoom lit up like a Christmas tree, her eyes glittering as we stepped off the stairs and into the dining room. She turned to face me, pinched my cheek. "Vay, cheghad dokhtareh nazi hasteetoh." *My, what a sweet, darling girl you are.*

Never mind, it had backfired.

"Dariush," she said, calling for her husband. "Bodo biyah. Shadi bidareh." *Come quickly. Shadi is awake.*

Agha—*Mister*—Dariush, as I called him, hurried into the living room, smiling and saying hello with a level of fanfare and enthusiasm that left me painfully embarrassed. I felt flush with joy and horror, unsure what to do with myself. Their kindness was too much, an overcorrection, but I actually believed them when they said they'd missed me. I felt it like a dart to the heart.

"Thank you. Thank you. But I should go," I tried again. "Please, really, I'm so grateful, thank you—I'm so sorry for troubling you—but I really, truly—"

"Khob, ghaza bokhoreem?" Zahra's dad cut me off with a wink and a smile, clapped his hands together. *So, should we eat?*

My heart sank.

He frowned, looked around. "Fereshteh," he said, "Ali kojast?" *Where's Ali?*

Fereshteh khanoom was standing in the kitchen, pulling plates out of a cupboard. She didn't even look up when she started shouting his name. "Ali," she bellowed. Then, in Farsi: "The food is getting cold!"

"Fereshteh khanoom," I said, trying, one last time, to exit stage left without insulting them. It was the height of cruelty to refuse them the chance to feed me—practically a sin—and I knew it. They knew it. And they weren't letting me off the hook. "Please," I said. "You've already done so much. I'm so grateful. Mozahemetoon nemikham besham." *I don't want to be a burden.*

"Boro beshin, azizam," she said, shoving a plate in my hands. *Go sit down, my love.* "I already called your mother. I told her you'd be having dinner here tonight."

A violent fear briefly paralyzed me.

She'd called my mother. *Of course she'd called my mother.*

My smile slipped and Fereshteh khanoom caught it, point oh five seconds of weakness and she caught it, her eyes narrowing at my face.

"I didn't tell her what happened," she said quietly, still speaking in Farsi. "But before the end of this night, you are going to tell *me*. Do you understand?"

My chest was heaving. I felt suddenly faint.

"Shadi. Look at me."

I met her eyes. She must've seen something in my face then, because the hard edge to her expression melted away. She set the stack of plates on the table. Took my hands in hers.

"Don't be afraid," she whispered. "It's going to be okay."

Heat, heat, rising up my chest, pushing against my throat, singeing my eyes.

I said nothing.

Fereshteh khanoom was still holding my hands when she suddenly turned her head toward the stairs. "Ali," she shouted. "For the love of your mother, come downstairs! Your food has frozen solid."

So, too, had my limbs.

TWENTY-ONE

When Zahra arrived, I was surprised.

Confused.

She froze in the doorway when she saw me, her eyes giving away her shock, then disappointment. I saw her glance at the clock in the living room. Glance at her mother.

"Bea beshin, Zahra," her mother said evenly. *Come sit down.*

That was when I understood.

Zahra had known I was here. She'd known and she'd left on purpose to avoid me, had estimated my hour of departure incorrectly. What I didn't understand was why she wasn't in class, where the both of us were supposed to be—and as my mind worked desperately to solve this riddle, I struck gold.

A memory.

The recollection was faint, but certain: a faded syllabus, a blur of due dates. There was some kind of school-wide event today, something teachers were required to attend. Classes had long ago been canceled. The professor had mentioned it on the first day—he'd told us to highlight the date, make note of it in our calendars.

I couldn't believe it.

The serrated edge of hope was pressing against my sternum, threatening, threatening. I felt, suddenly, like I couldn't breathe. This had been my single stroke of good luck in months.

I wasn't going to fail my class.

Tears pricked at my eyes just as Zahra mumbled hello, kicked off her shoes. Fereshteh khanoom shot me a look as I blinked away the emotion, and it didn't even bother me that she misunderstood. I'd shed many tears over Zahra; there was no falsehood in that. I tried not to watch her as she dumped her backpack next to mine on the living room couch, but I still saw her out of the corner of my eye. She said something about using the bathroom and promptly disappeared, never once glancing in my direction.

I stared at my plate, heat creeping up my face.

I wasn't welcome here. I'd known I wasn't welcome here. I wanted to tell Zahra as much, that I knew it and that I didn't mean to be here, that none of this had been intentional. It was a horrible series of accidents, I wanted to say to her. One mistake after another.

I would've left, I wanted to leave, they wouldn't let me, I wanted to scream.

I'd been sitting at this dinner table for forty minutes, answering a barrage of questions against my will, and I couldn't take much more. It would've been hard enough explaining my mother's panic attack, the many ambulances, my father's heart attacks—his surgeries, near misses with death, an unfulfilled promise to come home—with only Zahra's parents to judge and analyze. That Ali had been sitting at the table the whole time, refusing to look away from me as I spoke, was more than I could handle. I couldn't tear open my heart in front of Zahra, too.

Worse: they weren't done interrogating me.

I hadn't wanted to tell them about all the hours—the year—my mother had spent crying. I couldn't tell them she'd been self-harming. I didn't tell them what the doctor said, didn't tell them that I broke down her door this morning. I didn't want to give away her secrets; I knew she'd never forgive me. But I had to share part of it, haltingly, with difficulty, in order to explain why I'd passed out at school today—and why I'd begged the nurse not to call my mother. Still, they'd found my answers insufficient.

But why? they wanted to know. *Why? Why?*

"Yes—but why?" agha Dariush had asked. "She'd had a difficult night—bad news from your father, her reaction was understandable, especially after everything—but why wouldn't you call her? She'd want to know, azizam. She wouldn't want you to hide these things from her."

I shook my head, said nothing.

Fereshteh khanoom cleared her throat. "Okay. Basseh," she'd said. *Enough.* "Chai bokhoreem?" *Should we have tea?*

We'd not yet answered her question when Zahra arrived home.

We sat quietly at the table now, all of us staring at our plates while Zahra disappeared down the hall. We listened to the distant sounds of running water as she washed her hands, stalled for time. I knew she'd have to come out at some point, but I wasn't sure I wanted to be here when she did. I hadn't been prepared to face Zahra, not like this, not in front of her whole family.

I stood up suddenly.

"Please accept my apologies. I'm so grateful. You've been so kind. But I should go."

"You didn't even touch your food," Fereshteh khanoom cried. "You have to stay—you're wasting away. Smaller and smaller every time I see you." She turned to her husband. "Isn't it true? I don't like it."

"It's true," agha Dariush said, smiling at his wife. He turned to me. "You should eat more, Shadi joon. Just a little bit more, okay azizam? Beshin." *Sit.*

I stared at my full plate. I had no appetite.

"Please," I said, my voice practically a whisper. "Forgive me. I'm so sorry for intruding and for interrupting your day. I can't tell you how much I appreciate everything you've done for me—"

"There's no need." Agha Dariush cut me off with a tender smile. "We still have your letter, azizam. You don't need to thank us anymore."

"What letter?" were the first words Ali had spoken since he'd arrived downstairs.

I wanted, suddenly, to die.

That stupid letter. I was out of my mind when I wrote it. I'd been delirious with insomnia for days, trapped under a vicious grief, the waking nightmare that was my life. My brother was dead. My parents were killing each other. Every night my father would fall to his knees begging, begging like a child before a strange, hysterical version of my mother. She'd cry when she slapped him. She'd slap him and scream at him and he'd say nothing, do nothing, not even when she collapsed, dragging her fingernails down her own face.

I didn't sleep for four days.

I'd lie awake in bed imagining my mother curled on the floor of my brother's bedroom begging God to kill her and I couldn't breathe, couldn't close my eyes. When I finally collapsed at school I'd been so grateful for the reprieve, so grateful for the few hours of peace and comfort Zahra's parents provided that it nearly broke me. I didn't know why I'd decided to immortalize those feelings in a letter, the ghost of which kept haunting me. I didn't want anyone else to see it. I thought I would actually self-immolate if Ali read that letter.

Fereshteh khanoom made a sound—a sharp *eh*—something like irritation. It was a sound I'd heard a hundred other Iranian parents make when they were frustrated. "Why'd you say anything about her letter?" she snapped at her husband in Farsi. "Now you've embarrassed her."

"I really should go," I managed to choke out. "Please. I should get home."

Fereshteh khanoom shook her head at her husband. "Didi chikar kardi?" *Do you see what you did?*

"Hey," Ali said, looking at his parents. "What letter?"

"Oh, this was months ago," his mom said.

"How the hell is that an answer?"

"Don't say *hell* to your mother," agha Dariush said sharply, pointing his fork at his son.

Fereshteh khanoom smacked Ali on the arm. "Beetarbiat." *No manners.*

He rolled his eyes. "Can someone please just tell me what this letter is?"

"I have to go," I said desperately. "Please. I've infringed upon your kindness enough."

"Mashallah, she's so articulate, *nah?*" Agha Dariush beamed at his wife. "'Infringed' khaylee loghateh khoobiyeh." *"Infringed" is such a good word.*

"Jesus Christ," Ali muttered.

His mother hit him again.

Agha Dariush looked up at me then, put me out of my misery. "Of course you can go, azizam. You must want to get home to your mother."

"Yes, thank you."

"Ali," he said to his son. "Pasho." *Get up.*

To me, he said: "Ali will drive you home."

Ali pushed back his chair too quickly, wood screeching against wood so hard he nearly knocked over his seat. I watched as Fereshteh khanoom stared at him in surprise, studied his face with a sudden, dawning comprehension that drove the fear of God into my heart.

"No," I said quickly. "That's okay. I can walk home."

"It's freezing outside," Ali said, half shouting the words.

I looked at him, felt my heart quicken. Turned away.

"I like the cold," I said to his father. "But thank you for the offer."

"You don't even have a coat," Ali said. "Why do you never have a coat?"

"Yanni chi, *never?*" Agha Dariush was looking at his son like he'd lost his mind. "If she wants to walk home, let her walk home."

"Shadi, why won't you let me drive you home?"

I couldn't believe it. I couldn't believe Ali was doing nothing to conceal his frustration. I couldn't believe he wouldn't pretend, for five more seconds, in front of his family. It was as if he didn't know—or perhaps didn't care—that his mother was watching, seeing everything.

"I only live four streets away," I said, inching backward.

"You live half a mile from here."

"I don't—" I swallowed, grew flustered. Zahra had

reappeared at the dinner table, and she did not look happy. "I'll just, I'm sorry, I—"

"Wait," he said, "at least let me give you a jacket—"

"I'm sorry," I said, staring at the carpet. "Forgive me. Thank you for dinner. It was delicious. I'm sorry."

I nearly ran to the door.

TWENTY-TWO

Dear Fereshteh khanoom and agha Dariush,

Thank you for picking me up from school today. I didn't think anyone would come for me. You were so kind. You bought me medicine and let me sleep in your house, and agha Dariush made me a sandwich and I think it was the best sandwich I've ever eaten. I think Zahra is the luckiest person in the whole world to have you for parents, and I hope she knows how wonderful you are, that you are special parents, that not all parents are like you, and that she is very, very blessed to have you. I don't know what would've happened to me today if you hadn't come for me, and I'm so grateful. It had been a very hard day but you made it so much better, and I will always remember today, I will always remember how you treated me, and how you didn't get upset with me for not using the medicine you bought. I hope it wasn't very expensive. I will always be grateful to you and I pray that God blesses you and your family for your kindness, and for your generous hearts, and I hope I will know you forever.

Thank you again for everything. Thank you for being kind to me, and thank you to Fereshteh khanoom for letting me borrow some of Zahra's clothes, I will wash them and return them as soon as possible.

God bless you,

Shadi

I walked home hunched over, huddled into myself. I'd left my jacket in my locker and had never returned to school to grab it, and I was sorry to admit that Ali was right. It was freezing.

I shoved my hands in my pockets, looked up at the dark sky, prayed it wouldn't rain. My fingers closed, suddenly, around a piece of paper.

I stopped in the middle of the sidewalk, tugged it free. It was a poor rectangle, folded hastily. I pried it open, smoothed it out.

It was a form.

Something from the nurse's office—the kind of thing students were asked to fill out upon arrival—but this one was blank. There was no information, not even my own name, just a scribble across the bottom with a phone number and a brief message:

Call me when you wake up, okay? I'd like to make sure you're not dead. (This is Noah.)

I surprised myself when I smiled.

I was shivering in the cold without a jacket, terrified about the future, but I was smiling. It felt strange. I didn't know what to do about anything these days—not about my mom, who wouldn't accept professional help, not about my classes or my looming college applications, and not about my father, who may or may not have been dying.

I didn't know what to do about Ali.

I didn't know what was waiting for us or what the future might hold, whether it would hold us at all. Still, I felt a burgeoning hope when I thought of him, felt it push through the pain. I felt, for the first time, like one of the raging fires in my life had snuffed out.

I'd apologized.

Not long ago I thought I'd have to live my entire life plagued by the drumbeat of a single regret. Not long ago I thought Ali would never speak to me again. Not long ago I thought I'd lost forever something I knew now to be precious. Rare.

I looked up then, searched the sky.

When I found the moon I found God, when I saw the stars I saw God, when I let myself be inhaled by the vast, expanding universe, I understood God the way Seneca once did—*God is everything one sees and everything one does not see.*

I did not often believe in men, but I always believed in more.

The God I knew had no gender, no form. Islam did not accept the personification of God, did not believe in containing God. The common use of *he* as a pronoun was an error of translation.

There was only *they*, the collective *we*, the idea of infinity.

I'd always seen religion as a rope, a tool to help us grow nearer to our own hearts, to our place in this universe. I did not understand those who would malign, without forgiveness or empathy, others who did not conform to a series of static rules—rules that were never meant to inspire competition, but to build us up, make us better. Such moral superiority was antithetical to the essence of divinity, to the point of faith. It was made clear, time and time again, that it was not our place to exercise harsh, human judgment over those whose hearts we did not know. It was made unequivocally clear in the Qur'an that there should be no compulsion in religion.

And yet.

We were all of us lost.

When I pushed open the front door, I realized two things simultaneously:

First, that I'd left my backpack—my stupid, cumbersome, ridiculous backpack—at Zahra's house, which meant that if I wanted to have any chance of ever catching up on my homework, I'd have to go back and get it, the mere idea of which sent a chill through my heart.

And second—

Second, I realized my father was home.

My first clue were his shoes, sitting neatly by the door, the familiar pair of brown leather loafers I hadn't seen in weeks. My second clue was the smell of olive oil, chopped onions, sautéed beef, and the soft, sweet smell of fresh, sleeping rice. I heard the sound of my sister's voice, a peal of laughter.

Quietly, I shut the door behind me, and the scene came suddenly into view.

My mother was in the kitchen, stirring a pot of food made with ingredients that, just hours ago, had not existed in our cupboards. My father was sitting in a chair at the dining table, looking bone-weary but happy, his face older than I remembered it, his hair grayer. Shayda was sitting in a chair next to him, holding one of his hands in both of hers. She looked close to tears but lovely, her dark hair framing her face, her wide brown eyes rich with emotion. I seldom understood my sister, and did not understand her then, either. I didn't know how she could love a complicated man without it complicating her love. I didn't know how her mind sorted and prioritized emotion; I didn't know how she'd landed here—looking incandescent—after all we'd been through.

I realized then that it was none of my business.

I had no right to drag Shayda down with me. Had no right to steal the joy from her body. It was not my fault that I could not bend my heart to behave as hers did, and it was not her fault that she couldn't do the same for me.

I supposed we really were just different, in the end.

My father was the first to notice me.

He stood up too fast, gripped the table for support. Shayda cried out a warning, worried, and my father didn't seem to notice. His face changed as he took me in, studied my eyes. *His eyes.* He looked away, looked back, seemed to understand that I hated him, loved him.

Hated him.

I didn't even realize I was crying until he came forward on slow, unsteady legs, didn't realize I was sobbing until he pulled me into his arms. I cried harder when he became real, his arms real, his shape real, his body real. I cried like the child I was, like the child I wanted to be. I'd missed him, missed my horrible father, missed the way it felt to be held like this, to press my face against his chest, to inhale his familiar scent. He smelled like flowers, like rain, like leather. He smelled like exhaust fumes and coffee and paper. He was a horrible person, a wonderful person. He was cold and stupid and funny.

I hated him.

I hated him as he held me, hated him as I cried. The man who'd once felt to me like a solid block of concrete felt suddenly like blown glass, papier-mâché. I felt his arms shaking. Felt the cold, papery skin of his hands against my face as he pulled back, looked at me.

I couldn't meet his eyes.

I looked away, looked down, looked over his shoulder. My mother and sister were watching us closely, the two of them standing side by side in the kitchen. I stared at my mother, her hands clenching a towel, tears streaming down her face.

"Shadi," my father said quietly.

I looked up.

He smiled, his skin wrinkling, his eyes shining. He pulled me close again, wrapped me against his insubstantial figure. I could feel his ribs under my hands. Could count them. He spoke to me then, spoke in Farsi, pressed his cheek against my head.

"God alone," he said, his voice shaking, "God alone knows the depth of my regrets."

TWENTY-THREE

I ran through the night on shaking legs, tore through gusts of wind, propelled myself through the freezing cold by sheer force of will. I wanted to run forever, wanted to fling myself into orbit, wanted to drive my body into the ground. My skin was crawling with unspent emotion, the sensations spiraling up my back, skittering through my head.

I wanted to scream.

I'd run out the door based on a pretense, the pretense that I'd left my backpack at Zahra's house and needed to get it back, a pretense that held weight only as a result of Zahra's mom having called my mom to inform her that I'd had dinner there that night.

It has all my homework in it, I'd said. *I'll just be gone for a little while.*

A different version of me had used a similar excuse a

thousand times to buy myself more time away from these walls, from the suffocating sorrow they contained. I was always inventing reasons to spend longer at Zahra's house so I wouldn't have to be trapped in the amber of my own home and my parents knew this, had always seen through me. They probably knew I was up to no good even now, but perhaps they'd also seen something in my face, understood how I might be feeling, that I needed to leave. Run for my life.

Reluctantly, suspiciously, my parents let me go.

I ran.

I ran through the night on burning legs, with burning lungs, dragged air into my chest with difficulty. My limbs were trembling, my body shutting down.

I pushed harder.

I let the wind sear my skin, let it whip the tears from my eyes. I let the cold numb my nose, my chin, the tips of my fingers, and I ran, ran through darkness, chest heaving, breaths ragged.

I collapsed when I got to the park, my knees sinking into wet grass. I rested for only a moment, body bowed halfway to prostration before I pushed myself up again, dragged myself across an open field. When I saw the shimmering lights in the distance, I realized I knew what I wanted to do. I also knew then that Shayda had been right.

I'd probably lost my mind.

The gate was locked so I jumped the fence, landed poorly. Pain shot up my leg and I welcomed it, ignored it.

As I stood, I stalled.

I caught my breath, stared. There was no one here. There was never anyone here. I'd walked past this pool a thousand times on similar evenings, wondering always at the effort expended to maintain such a place for the mere mice and ghosts who haunted it.

The light was ethereal here, bright and glowing, the glittery depths swaying a little in the wind. I had no plan. I had no exit strategy. I had no way of knowing how I'd get home or in what state. I only knew I felt my chest heaving, my bones heavy with ice and heat. I was sweating and freezing, fully clothed, desperate for something I could not explain.

I kicked off my shoes. Tore off my jacket.

Dove into the water.

I sank. Closed my eyes and sank.

Screamed.

Silk wrapped around my head and I screamed, tore the sorrow from my lungs, water filling my mouth. I screamed and nearly choked in the effort, thought it might kill me. The water absorbed me instead, swallowed my pain, kept my secrets.

Let me drown.

I kicked up suddenly, struggled as my clothes grew heavy. I broke the surface with a gasp, drank in the cool night air, swallowed untold amounts of chlorinated water. The pool was unexpectedly warm, welcoming, like a bath. I took a deep, steadying breath. Another.

Sank back down.

I listened to the whir of silence, to the thick, distant thuds of water. I let myself fall, let my weight drag me down.

It was somehow a comfort not to breathe.

I sat at the bottom of the pool and the water compressed me, held me with its heft. Slowly, my heartbeat began to steady.

The home I'd run from tonight had been warm, hopeful—unrecognizable from what it had become in the last year. Until tonight I'd never even considered we might be happy again; I'd never dreamed we might use the broken pieces of our old life to build something new. I'd thought, for so long, that this pain I clenched every day in my fist would be my sole possession, all I ever carried for the rest of my life.

I'd forgotten I had two hands.

I felt a key click into the clockwork of my heart then, felt a terrifying turning in my chest that promised to keep me going, to buy me more time in this searing life. I felt it, felt my body restart with a climbing, aching fear. I feared that something was changing, that maybe I was changing, that my entire life was shedding a skin it had outgrown at last, at last.

It scared me.

I didn't know how to handle the shape of hope. I didn't know how such a thing might fit in my body. I was so afraid, so afraid of being disappointed.

I felt him before I saw him, arms around my body, a blur of movement, shuddering motion. The world came back to me in an explosion of sound, heaving breaths and cool air, the shaking of branches, whispering leaves. I was gasping, clinging to the slick edge of the pool, my thin clothes painted to my body, my scarf suctioned to my head.

I dragged myself out of the water, collapsed sideways. I was breathing hard, staring up at the sky. I could feel my heart pounding, my pulse racing.

"Sometimes, I swear, I really think you're trying to kill me."

I pulled myself up at the sound of his voice, bent my sopping knees to my chest. Ali was sitting at the edge of the pool, his legs still in the water, his body drenched. I watched him as he stared into the glowing depths, his hands planted on either side of him. Rivulets of water snaked down his face. He was beginning to shiver.

"What are you doing here?"

He turned to look at me. "Are you?" he asked. "Are you trying to kill me?"

"No," I whispered.

"I went to your house," he said. "You forgot your backpack in my living room. But when I got there your mom told me you'd gone to get it yourself, she said that maybe I'd missed you on the way over."

I sighed, stared into the water. "How'd you know I was here?"

"I didn't. I searched the park. I saw your shoes through the fence." He nodded at the bars around the community swimming pool. "So I jumped it. God, Shadi, I didn't know what you were doing." He dropped his face in his hands. Pushed wet hair out of his eyes. "You scared the shit out of me."

"What did you think I was doing?"

"I don't know," he said, exhaling suddenly. "I don't know."

I knew.

I picked up my sopping self, dripped over to him, sat down beside him. I noticed then that his fists were clenched. His body was shaking.

"Come on," I said softly, tugging at his arm. "You're freezing. You have to go home. You have to get dry."

"*Shadi.*"

I hesitated at the sound of his voice. He sounded raw, close to pain. He turned, I turned, I searched his eyes. I saw something in his face that scared me, sent my heart racing. I touched his cheek almost without meaning to, traced the curve of his cheekbone. He sighed, the sound scattered.

"What are we doing?" he whispered.

I felt something snap inside of me, felt something sever. I stared at him with a trembling hope. My soggy mind didn't know what it was doing. My own name pressed against my tongue.

Shadi meant *joy*, and all I ever did was cry.

Ali touched my chin, grazed my lips with his fingers. "Do you know what my mom said to me when you left?"

I shook my head.

"She was like, *Ali, you idiot, that girl will never be interested in you. You don't even know how to talk to girls like that. She's way too good for you.*"

I almost laughed. I felt closer to crying.